Nyifie Brothers Publishing

FAT VAMPIRE 4

Harder Better Fatter Stronger

JOHNNY B. TRUANT

BIG PUSSY

Greta walked into Reginald's room in the catacombs beneath the Chateau de Differdange holding a pickle in one hand and a coffee cup filled with blood in the other. She stood in the doorway, watching Reginald with a sympathetic expression on her face, and then dunked the pickle as if it were a long green donut. It came out as red as a fat tube of lipstick. Carefully holding the pickle above the cup to catch errant drips, Greta took a bite. Her fangs were out. The pickle crunched.

"I'm glad you're here, Greta," said Reginald. "Next to the things you eat, my Twinkies and microwave pizzas look downright normal."

Greta looked down, rubbing the basketball-sized lump under the front of her shirt. "Claus vants it," she said in a thick Zsa Zsa Gabor accent. "I don't even like pickles."

As if in answer, a voice spoke up from under Greta's shirt. It wasn't a real voice, of course. Nobody could hear it other than Greta and Reginald, both of whom heard it telepathically. But still, in Reginald's head, the voice sounded real. Specifically, it sounded like Colonel Klink from *Hogan's Heroes*.

Greta's belly said, *Reginaaald! Let's watch some pooorn!*

Listening, Reginald felt himself transported back in time, television-wise. Claus even had Colonel Klink's vocal inflections right.

But then, before Reginald could answer re: watching porn so that a three hundred and ninety year-old vampire fetus could psychically sample it, Greta slapped her stomach in admonition.

"Claus!" she shouted. "Vat goes into you goes into me, and I am tired of your gross porn!"

The voice said, *I... know... NOTHING!*

But because Claus's response didn't make sense and because he didn't understand how blood ties worked, Reginald wondered again whether he might be projecting personality onto the fetus that wasn't actually there. Maybe Claus sounded entirely different to Greta. Maybe he fed her entirely different nostalgic catch phrases. Reginald wondered if imagining a German baby as sounding like Klink made him racist.

Greta turned to Reginald. "I am sorry, Reginald," she said. "He can be so immature sometimes."

Reginald, who wondered how it would feel to spend four centuries floating in amniotic fluid while nursing a rather divergent sex addiction, said nothing.

Greta walked to the side of Reginald's bed and eased herself into a chair. Her movements were slow and deliberate, but familiar. She'd forgotten what it was like to not be pregnant. Over the years, her vampire back had strengthened, and she no longer felt pains. She no longer remembered how to walk with a non-pregnant gait. Stumbling along and sitting awkwardly in chairs and dripping blood on her stomach because she couldn't get close to tables had become the norm.

"You shouldn't just stay in here and mope," said Greta. "You zit here and you eat and you vatch movies on your computer. But zis is no way for a vampire to live. You don't have to hunt with the others. Ve know you aren't a good hunter. But you can at least sit vith us. You can join us in the cathedral room and socialize. You can be part of this family. Karl vants to hear vhat you have to say. Ve all do. Especially now."

Reginald rolled over to face the wall, away from Greta.

"I'm in hiding," he grunted. "It's like mourning, except that you get to watch slapstick comedies." But now that he thought about it, watching those comedies wasn't always a "get to" situation. Last night he'd watched *Dumb and Dumber* and had wished that it was still possible to die.

"I understand. But Reginald, you are being a pussy."

Reginald turned to look at Greta. That had gotten his attention.

They'd been at the Chateau for almost three months. During that time, the European Vampire Council and the others living under the Chateau had treated Reginald, Maurice, and Nikki like visiting dignitaries who'd just watched their families murdered. They'd been welcomed in, and then they'd been given as much time and space as they needed to recover from leaving everything behind in America. Nikki and Maurice took a week to mope, then donned their optimist hats and began making themselves at home, clubbing and dining on the locals. Reginald, by contrast, was still wearing his "why the hell should I bother" hat. And also his "fuck off; I'm eating" pajamas.

"I'm sorry," said Reginald. "Is my presence in my own room distracting to you?"

"Someone needs to tell you zat you are being a whiny pussy. Your friends will not, so I will. You cannot be mad at a pregnant girl."

"I can try," said Reginald.

Greta eyed him. Then, after staring into her green eyes for twenty uncomfortable seconds, Reginald turned back to face the wall.

It didn't matter. None of it mattered. Maurice would never be recognized as Deacon of the American Council again. The vampire government's infrastructure was continuing to crumble. Reginald had peeked into the Council's computer systems a few times since arriving in Luxembourg (hacking was easy when you had a genius mind) and had discovered that none of the relocation or protection systems were in place anymore. The vampire social networks, however, were booming. Fangbook was more active than ever, and new videos of vampire atrocities — as well as insider looks into the combination slaughterhouse / puppet show that the Council had become — were posted every minute. It was too sad to watch. The chaos, panic, and murder were too widespread, too popular, too accepted. The old Council, under Logan, had ruled by fear. Now, under Barkley, it ruled by indifference. Without direction from above, the citizenry was like tens of thousands of unguided missiles: they blew up what they wanted when they wanted, and the world was paying the price.

Speaking to the wall, Reginald said, "Why bother to discuss it, Greta? I can't go home. None of us can. America is eating itself alive, quite literally. With Charles in charge..." Then he stopped and laughed out loud.

"What?"

Reginald turned. "I just said 'Charles in Charge.' "

Greta just stared at him. She didn't get it.

"I'm just saying there's no point," said Reginald. "America is fucked. The rest of the world might hang in there for a little while, but eventually it'll spread and then we'll be fucked, too."

"So you're giving up?"

Reginald fluffed a pillow and studied the stone wall in front of him. "Yep."

In a way, the disintegration of the vampire world was a relief to Reginald. He hadn't felt comfortable as a human, but he felt even less comfortable as a slow, weak vampire who couldn't catch prey and who didn't like to drink blood. With only a very few exceptions, he loathed vampires. Most were murderous, bullying, elitist thugs. The fact that the vampires' creators seemed likely to eliminate the entire race at any time might actually be a good thing. Sure, he'd die. And Nikki would die. And Maurice would die. And his few friends under the Chateau would die. But the humans would be safe.

And in truth, there weren't many humans that Reginald cared about, either. He cared about his mother despite her passive-aggressiveness, and he cared about Nikki's sister because she mattered to Nikki. But mostly, Reginald cared about Claire.

Claire, who was only a little girl.

Claire, who still had her whole life in front of her.

Claire, who was still out there, unprotected, in the warzone.

Reginald worried ceaselessly about Claire. Before boarding their plane to New York, the three refugees had picked up two humans and a vampire to bring with them as protected guests: Maurice's wife, Reginald's mother, and Nikki's sister. They'd run together to Claire's house, each of the strong vampires carrying a human or Reginald. They'd knocked. They'd rung the doorbell. They'd shouted. Reginald tried to enter the house, but found that his invitation had been revoked. For a while, they'd thought that Claire and Victoria weren't home (despite the fact that the hospital had released Victoria following her near-death at the hands of vampire assailants), but then a small, female voice had called to them from the center of the house. It had repeated the revocation of all three of their invitations, then had told them to leave... that the poor little humans would be fine without their protection.

Reginald had tried to protest, but time was short — the Council and Guards were probably looking for them at that very moment — so Maurice had seized him bodily and had dragged him away. A half hour later, two humans and four vampires were being packed into a crate. Seventeen hours after that, they were in the catacombs under the Chateau de Differdange in the duchy of

Luxembourg, leaving Claire and Victoria back in the States as two big, flapping loose ends.

"It's been three months," said Greta. "You can't just continue to mope."

"Sure I can," said Reginald. "Look, I'll show you." He wedged his bulk more securely in the corner.

Behind him, Reginald heard Greta stand. She sighed. "Suit yourself, pussy," she said. Then, after a moment, he could tell by the empty sound of the room and the change in psychic presence that she had gone.

Reginald laid on his side and stared at the wall. Like those in all of the rooms below the Chateau, the wall was raw stone that had been sprayed with a sealant to keep the rooms dry and to keep rock dust from crumbling in. Reginald let the rock be his world for the moment. It was easier that way. The rock expected nothing from him. The rock didn't change from day to day. The rock, thanks to its spray-seal, didn't disintegrate and fall apart and threaten to crush them all. The rock was uncomplicated and simple. Sure the rock was boring, but at least it wasn't being led into chaos by a psychopath.

Light footsteps appeared behind Reginald.

"Babe," said a soft voice.

Nikki.

In a moment, she'd touch his shoulder. She'd ask him how he was doing. She'd try and convince him to come join the others. He'd refuse, citing his total lack of interest in continuing to force a solution onto a hopeless problem. He'd say that he'd rather just sit in his room and wait for the world to end, watching TV and eating Cheetos. And because she loved him, she'd let him do it.

Instead of putting her hand gently on Reginald's shoulder, Nikki punched the back of his head hard enough to drive his face two inches into the rock in front of him, pulverizing the front of his skull. Then, once his neck healed enough to allow it, Reginald pulled his face from the rock crater and turned. He looked at her, hurt.

Nikki was behind him, tall and strong and beautiful, wearing all black like a vampire assassin — right down to the long leather boots with the high heels.

"I don't have time to play your self-pity game," she said. "Something is happening. Get up and follow me. Now."

When Reginald arrived in the cathedral room — a huge space at the foot of the staircase that led to the castle above — he found EU Deacon Karl Stromm staring at a huge flat computer monitor. Karl did not look up. The other members of the Council were clustered around him, also staring at the screen. At first Reginald was intrigued, wondering what breaking story they might be watching unfold, but when he hooked around the group to peer at the monitor for himself, he was underwhelmed. It was the same old thing as always: a live, static shot from the American Vampire Council's lone remaining security camera.

Onscreen, a few dangerous and dirty-looking groups of vampires milled through the arena. The floor was littered with human bodies and drenched with blood. Reginald could also see piles of ash that had once been vampires, indicating that there had been little prejudice in recent killings. The very walls of the arena were dented and battered, but the location still seemed to be the subbasement under the Asbury Club. That would mean that the Council hadn't relocated in almost four months. None of this was good news.

Reginald located Maurice, who was seated at the back of the

small cluster, and dragged a small plastic chair over from the wall to sit next to him. The chair was bright blue and had been brought down from the school above when the American group had arrived. The chair's legs groaned as Reginald sat. Nikki pulled up a second chair and sat next to him, rubbing his shoulder in silent apology for the harsh way she'd gotten his attention back in the room.

Then, as Reginald watched the monitor, the floor of the American Council began to fill. The bloody pools vanished beneath the crowd's feet. The scarred walls were blocked by bodies. Within a few minutes, vampires were everywhere — standing, walking, even climbing the walls — all looking forward, all curiously quiet. They seemed to be looking at the Deacon's box.

Reginald leaned forward and put a hand on Karl's shoulder.

"What's going on?" he asked.

Karl turned. He was wearing a dramatic cloak made of red silk interwoven with gold fibers. His black hair was in a pony tail, held in place by a carved ring of wood.

"Charles is speaking," he said, his voice full of old-world affect. "Some think this is when he officially takes control, naming himself Deacon."

Reginald sat back, crossing his arms. "It's just a formality. Charles has been the unofficial Deacon for months." He turned to Nikki. "You smashed my face into the wall for this?"

"Not for *Charles*," said Karl. "I tell her to summon you because of this." He reached into a pocket in his robes, pulled out a cell phone, pressed a few buttons, and handed it back over his shoulder to Reginald. It was a casual series of movements, but Reginald still found it all very strange coming from Karl. Karl's usual demeanor was like something from medieval times. Getting an iPhone from him was like receiving a text message from Count Dracula.

On the phone's screen was an email. Reginald read it and then handed the phone back, having committed every pixel of the message to memory.

"Who is Nicholas Timken?" he asked.

"He is a frequent visitor to the Chateau before, when Maurice and Logan were Deacon. *Amerikaner*. He came each year for Oktoberfest and stayed with us. He contacted me after you came here and has been like eyes and ears for us."

Reginald gestured at the screen. "We already have eyes and ears."

"Nicholas feels like Maurice does," Karl continued, ignoring the interruption. "He has no love for Council, but he sees what will happen if there is no Council, or if Charles takes over, which is like the same thing. We here could survive without a government because we are old and know the old ways. But in America?" Karl shrugged to indicate that America was filled with douchebags, which Reginald found himself unable to completely disagree with. "He says he wants to find a solution. I guess he must have found it."

"And he seems like a bit of a drama queen," Reginald added. Timken's email to Karl was brief and unnecessarily mysterious. It said, *Watch the Council video feed at 0:00 GMT.* He could easily have told his European allies what he was up to, but apparently he wanted to put on a show instead. Reginald looked at an ancient-looking clock built into the room's stone wall. The hands stood at 12:55am local time. Five minutes left.

Nikki was clicking around on her laptop, which she'd plugged into the Chateau's network.

"Hey, there's a first-person feed," she said. "Check it out; someone in the crowd is streaming video." She turned her screen to show the others, but Reginald found the presence of a live stream in the crowd odd. It couldn't be a random person with a cell phone, because the Council structure blocked cellular signals. The camera would have to be hard-wired. But after displaying stupidity and apathy about everything else, why would Charles suddenly think to plant a camera in the crowd?

Karl squinted at Nikki's laptop, then typed a new address into the computer in front of him. The view on the large monitor became the same as on Nikki's screen: a close-up shot of the Deacon's box. The camera zoomed in. The box was no longer empty; several vampires milled at its back, shuffling papers. Then one of the vampires turned and approached the front of the box. It was Charles.

Charles was dressed in formal black robes that were a total departure from his usual pressed slacks and designer shirts. His face looked serious and determined. He was holding a stack of papers. The papers looked as odd in his hands as the robe looked on his shoulders; Charles wasn't organized or official or any of the other things that paperwork usually connoted. He should have been holding a man purse. Or a high-end vibrator from The Sharper Image, which he'd use as a combination come-on and conversation piece.

"He looks presidential, I'll give him that," said Reginald. "Or Deaconish. Whatever the term is."

Months ago, back when Maurice had made his final speech as Deacon — the speech after which the entire assembly had tried to kill him — he'd called for a leader to rise and take control of the Council. The Vampire Nation was descending into chaos, he said, and it needed a brain to steer it away from the abyss. Maurice had known that the leader that Council chose would probably be Charles. It was okay (though not ideal) because at the time, Charles had seemed better than leaderlessness... but in the intervening months, Maurice had begun to wonder. Reginald had begun to wonder, too.

Maurice shifted in his seat, then turned to Reginald. "We knew this was coming, but I still keep asking myself: 'Is it better to have a nation of vampires who kill and rampage at random, or a nation of vampires who kill and rampage under the direction of a total asshole?' "

"It's the eternal question," said Reginald. "Like the sound of one hand clapping."

"It sounds like this," said Nikki, turning and clapping her palm against the hand Reginald had extended.

"That's cheating."

"Yeah, well," said Nikki. "Armageddon and all."

Charles put his hands on the stone ledge around the Deacon's box, looking out across the assembly. He tapped the stack of papers on the ledge, then held them in front of his face. He was going to read his speech from them. Reginald couldn't help but feel annoyed. Couldn't Charles have bothered to memorize a speech? He was about to become the most powerful vampire in the western world, and he was totally phoning it in.

But then Charles held the papers over his head and tore them in half.

"Ah, very original," said Maurice. "Tearing paper. That means he's a rebel."

"Now he's going to say that old rules don't apply," said Nikki. "Just watch."

"The old rules of the Vampire Nation no longer apply," Charles said, his voice booming across the crowd.

Nikki raised an eyebrow at Maurice and Reginald.

"What a cock," said Maurice, staring daggers at the screen.

Karl shushed them.

But it was true, what Charles said. The old rules *didn't* apply. Under Logan, the Vampire Nation had been organized and efficient, but that had been before vampirekind had met its maker — quite literally — on a hilltop in Germany. Before the hilltop encounter, the most important issues in front of vampires had been feeding and sex and fashion. Today, after being handed the evolve-or-die edict, the key issue was survival itself. The problem was that everyone had different ideas of what "survive" meant.

Charles's idea seemed to involve forming gangs, killing, turning, and general mayhem.

In his mind, Reginald heard Claire saying, *There's a great change coming. A war, between humans and vampires.* Claire didn't think she'd been telling the future when she'd said that, but her blood and her pedigree suggested otherwise. And now, the changes at Council and the multiplying murders in the country's streets were bearing her out.

"Over the past year, we have been led by an impotent leader..." Charles said.

Maurice objected, adding that Charles should ask his mother if Maurice were impotent.

"... and during that time, we've lost our way. We've lost our identity. How many of you have begun to question your power since the Ring of Fire incident? How many of you have been afraid?" He didn't wait for the assembly to reply. Instead, he screamed, "*Why are you afraid? You are VAMPIRES!*"

The audience began to murmur its agreement.

"I have been trying to steer this Council back onto the tracks. I have been organizing our soldiers. I have been strategizing, not sitting on my hands. The Deacon of this Council is still, officially, Maurice Toussant. And today I ask you: do you want to allow him to *continue* to rule you... wherever he might be hiding?"

The crowd booed and jeered.

"I say it's time for a change!" Charles continued. "I say it's time to turn this Nation away from fear! I say that we..."

There was suddenly a loud banging noise and a flurry of activity. Every head in the room turned to look toward the back of the arena, away from Charles.

The camera swiveled.

The entrance to the Council chamber had blown open. The set of doors leading to the outside were mangled, with giant twisted holes where the locks used to be. Four rows of helmeted vampires wearing body armor were pouring into the room through the doors, taking up stations around the edges of the arena and pointing strange wand-like devices at the vampires in front of them. There were dozens of men rushing in, then scores, then hundreds. The flow was enormous, and soon the room was more helmets than hair and heads. All of the soldiers — they *had* to be soldiers — were dressed the same: each wore a bright red helmet bearing some sort of an insignia. Their armor and boots were black. The wand-like things they held were also black. Nobody seemed to know what the wands were, but all had concluded they were worth stepping away from, and they did, many with their hands up.

The camera swiveled to the Deacon's box. Charles and Todd Walker were still in the same positions, stock still, their eyes wide with shock.

The camera swiveled back, then panned the room.

Once the red-helmeted vampires were equally spaced around the arena, a final figure in the same gear marched through the mangled doors and headed for the center of the assembly. This one wasn't holding a wand, but the vampires parted in front of him anyway. But when the newcomer was halfway toward the middle of the room, a shout came from one of the corners. The camera jerked toward the noise. Several vampires had decided to seize one of the armored vampires, and the camera watched as one of the assembly members clung to the soldier's head and neck, trying to scratch and bite. Another vampire was wrapped around him, attempting to go for his legs.

There was a blue flash and a snapping noise like the pop of a bug zapper, and both of the attackers puffed into gray ash.

The red-helmeted vampire shrugged his shoulders, adjusting himself, and then resumed his post without ceremony: his back to the wall, his wand out. But fear had already started to spread, and the entire room began to shimmer with activity. Vampires, seeing what they were facing, began to panic. There was sparring and pushing and the blurring of motion. Another of the wand devices went off, and three more vampires on the opposite wall turned to ash. Vampires began to scream, to yell, to climb into the rafters. Everyone was rushing toward the doors.

But then there was another loud banging noise, this one deep like a cannon. Every vampire in the room froze. All heads — and the streaming video's frame — swiveled to focus on the man who had been walking to the center of the room. During the melee, he'd grabbed a chair and was standing atop it, holding a pistol over his head. The barrel smoked. Above him, rock dust filtered down from a bullet hole in the ceiling. He used his free hand to remove his helmet, revealing a head of short, blonde hair and a narrow, serious face. He tossed the helmet to one of the soldiers.

"The vampire revolution has broken out!" he yelled. "The hall is filled with six hundred men. Nobody is allowed to leave!"

Watching in the Chateau, Reginald leaned toward Karl's ear.

"Is that Timken?" he whispered.

A serious look on his face, without taking his eyes off the screen, Karl nodded.

Timken lowered the pistol and slipped it into a holster at his waist. Every eye was on him, including that of the camera. He met those eyes, looking around the room slowly, taking his time. The camera zoomed in, giving a nice close up. He looked neither nervous nor triumphant.

"This," said Timken, patting the pistol on his side and speaking in a loud, commanding voice, "is a regular gun with bullets tipped in silver. But in case anyone hasn't yet figured it out, the weapons in the hands of the Sedition Army are much more dangerous. They fire a high-pressure burst of silver particles, like a grenade that can be detonated over and over again. If one is fired near you and you aren't wearing gear, there's a good chance that a speck of sliver will penetrate your heart. And you've seen what happens then." He gestured toward the piles of ash.

He turned to face the camera. The shot was close, with good sound, and made Timken look both proud and unstoppable. Reginald found himself wondering if the cameraperson was a plant, placed in the assembly ahead of time.

"My name is Nicholas Timken," he said. "I lead this group in revolution over the established order of the defunct Vampire Council. We don't want to hurt anyone, but we will if we must. We are not, by nature, anarchists or subversionists. I am truly sorry that I have to introduce myself to the Vampire Nation this way. But my hand was forced. You see what this *'government'* has become." He said the word with venom, as if it were slimy to the touch.

Timken extended a hand toward the Deacon's box, where Barkley continued to stare. Several Sedition Army soldiers had come up behind him, their wands at the ready.

"You have before you Councilman Charles Barkley, who took the helm of this Nation as fear spread among our people. Then he fostered that fear, making it grow. And today, he wants to lead you legitimately. But his government — his 'legitimacy' as a leader — is a farce. I have tried to contact Mr. Barkley and those in his regime. I have tried diplomacy. I have pursued action via the normal legal channels, but the system has broken, and the channels have broken with them. My concerns have not been heard, and so in front of you all today, here they are."

Timken took a breath, stood taller.

"Councilman Barkley is a criminal! Your Deacon lives, yet Barkley has the audacity to tell you what to do. And look what you have done — what we have *all* done! — under that leadership. We have become animals! We hide in the sewers and we pop up like boogeymen, like carnival horrors. Did you know that the humans have been training forces to fight us for centuries? Did you know that only the most fragile balance keeps us from outright war? Did you know that we face a fight on two fronts — from the so-called 'fallen angels' on the right and the humans on the left? Of *course* you don't know those things. Mr. Barkley didn't tell you. Or perhaps, Barkley didn't understand himself that actions always have consequences. 'Smash and grab,' that's his plan... and damn the consequences.

"I have tried to make myself heard, for the good of us all. For the salvation — the *triumph!* — of our proud race. But I have been ignored. So today, I will not be ignored. I will tell you what Barkley has not, and it's this: the humans know we exist. Not all of them, of course, but a few that matter. And right now, thanks to Mr. Barkley's actions, a trained squad of killers known as the Anti-Vampire Taskforce is preparing to engage us. We cower from them. We cower from the Ring of Fire. We cower from all sides, like rats in a trap. Why?"

He took a slow, dramatic breath and scanned the room.

"Vampires of the proud Vampire Nation! You have lived like barbarians. You have resorted to an existence like that of animals. Is this how you wanted to spend your eternity? The day I became a vampire was the proudest day of my life. Was it yours? And if it was, is *this* the existence you asked for? Is *this* the future you want for yourself?"

Timken stopped talking, giving every vampire watching a few quiet moments to answer the questions for themselves. Nobody had been even reasonably content under Barkley. They had survived *despite* Barkley's incompetence.

The camera zoomed out, panning the room. The video drove home Timken's message: *This chaos, this destruction, this vagabond and barbarian life — this is what awaits you under Barkley's rule.*

"We have come in force, willing to kill every member of this Council and assembly if needed, because it was the only way to be heard, the only way to wrestle power from these barbarians. But this slippery descent into madness stops here. Starting today, this farce of a Council does not rule the Vampire Nation. *We* do. But this is not a takeover. We are not conquerors. We are mere stewards of the power that Barkley held. We will take these criminals into custody. We will clean up this structure. But then we will relinquish our throat-hold on this government and we will leave it to you — to the people of the proud Vampire Nation — to choose your own fate."

Murmurs began around the room. Even across the ocean, the vampires in the Chateau could sense the change in the room's mood.

"In one month's time, we will hold the free election that was never conducted when 'Councilman' Barkley and his cadre drove the Deacon out of power and attempted to assassinate him," said Timken. "And at that election, you may — if you wish — choose to elect Barkley as your Deacon. You may choose to keep me on as your leader. Or you may find another. I can promise you a smooth and fair transition of power into the hands that you choose."

Timken unholstered his pistol, then pointed it at Barkley. Barkley ducked, but Timken was merely using it to point, and to send a message.

"This ends tonight!" Timken shouted. "We are doing what needed to be done, and when we are finished, you will decide whether you want to live as cowards or rise as gods. The choice is yours."

Suddenly, Timken raised his gun hand over his head and fired another shot into the ceiling.

"I do what I do because we are vampire!" he boomed. *"And we deserve more than this!"*

BETTER OFF UNDEAD

The vampires in the cathedral room all began to talk at once. EU Council members turned to Maurice, asking if he knew Timken, if he'd known what was going to happen tonight, if this felt like justice to him. Others turned to Reginald and asked for his analysis: What did the overthrow mean? Was it bad because it was a coup, or good because that coup had ousted an incompetent tyrant? It was true, what Timken had said about the human shock troops; there was even a human/vampire summit in Paris in just a few days. Would Timken's overthrow help the spirit of the summit or harm it?

Karl, unreadable, began to stalk back and forth like an angry cat.

Reginald felt his head spin. He'd been diligently ignoring the outside world, and now he felt like he'd been beaten over the head with it. Not only had the changes in the Vampire Nation just ratcheted up a huge notch, but now everyone was coming to him — he with his unmatched vampire mind — for advice. He felt frozen and out of practice. He'd spent the last three months trying to kill that "unmatched vampire mind" with the numbest of inputs and the worst of foods, all the while refusing to drink enough of the blood it needed to function. For three months, all he'd thought about had been food and entertainment (and, when Nikki became horny enough for her lust to overcome her irritation, sex). And now this. *This* was his welcome-back puzzler.

Revolution. A *coup d'état*.

Reginald struggled to assimilate all of the details and decide: was this a necessary and righteous overthrow, or was it just more blood in the water?

Karl held his hands high. His red and gold robes swayed and opened beneath his arms like a cape.

"Quiet, quiet!" he yelled, his voice irritated. He squinted his eyes and pinched his forehead as if he had a headache. "Let's discuss this, but one at a time only. Obviously this changes things. But for the better or worse, I cannot say."

"Are you joking, Karl?" said a thin, beautiful woman with dark hair. It was Lola, the woman with whom the angel Santos had been infatuated. "It's *better*. How could it be worse? We couldn't so much as contact Barkley; we just had to watch him destroy America and wait for the chaos to spread here. But you *know* Timken. Now we have an open door to speak to America. Timken mentioned the AVT shock troops, so he understands what's at stake. He knows about the summit, and he knows you're attending it. Now they'll listen to reason. Now, they'll talk."

"I don't know," said Karl. "I don't know." He continued to pace, his eyes at his feet. "Reginald, you are the strategist. What do you think?"

But Reginald had no idea what to think. He'd spent too much time lying around on his ass and trying futilely to die. The only things he knew about the outside world were the few bits that Nikki told him while he watched downloaded movies on his computer and tried to ignore her.

"Charles didn't care about leading the Council," said Lola, speaking if Reginald wouldn't. "He only cared about having power. The only item on his agenda was satisfying the angels after the

Ring of Fire, but his solution was to kill and turn as many humans as possible. Reginald said that things on the streets were bad when you left. They must be much worse now. With Charles at the helm, America would have very quickly disintegrated into war. The walls of secrecy keeping vampires hidden and safe would fall. Gangs would roam the cities in the open, and in retaliation, humans would seek out and eliminate entire nests while the sun was out. The balance would swing back and forth with each cycle of the sun, with humans ruling the day and vampires ruling the night. The bloodshed would increase as each tried to outpace the other, the only question being who could do more damage with the half of the day they were given."

"So this is good," said Karl, still looking at Reginald and ignoring Lola.

But Reginald could only shake his head.

Karl continued to pace.

"Nicholas has been petitioning the Council for months, and they have been ignoring him," he said. "I have seen the frustration and the fury in his emails. He must have felt that this was the only way." Karl was talking to himself, seeming to think out loud. "Nicholas is an interesting fellow. His intentions usually seem noble, but he is so ambitious that it has always made me uneasy. But he says he will hold the elections. Maybe he means it. After all, Timken supported Maurice. He was one of the few. So maybe it is true. Maybe we have a new friend in America."

"He's not calling for Maurice's return, though," said Nikki.

"But he *is* calling for elections," said a thin vampire named Mellus.

"Which could be rigged," said Nikki.

Reginald looked over at Nikki. She'd been a vampire for nearly a year now, and the role fit her like a glove. It was hard to believe she'd ever been human. She was dark and beautiful and mysterious and quiet and moved like a panther. Her lips looked best with a pair of fangs.

"This was the only way and we all know it," said Mellus. "They would not listen to reason. In this case, a just and peaceful overthrow by a good vampire would look exactly the same as a power grab by a tyrant, so we can't tell them apart. At least Karl knows Nicholas. And no matter what we think, he is there now. It is *done*. We have to give him the benefit of the doubt."

"It was the only way," Lola agreed. "It took violence to fix what Charles was doing. Now Timken is there, but he's just a wartime leader, holding power until a suitable replacement can be found."

"Like Julius Caesar," said Nikki.

Mellus and Lola both shot her a look.

Reginald rubbed his forehead. He felt as if all of the abilities he'd developed over the past year had totally vanished: processing so fast that it was like stopping time, the ability to block pain, his balance and dexterity, his ability to influence blood relatives, and the sensed-but-still-hidden bomb that the angel Balestro had planted in his mind. He felt as if he was once again just a fat treadmill salesman, unable to defend himself against Todd Walker's mockery.

"We would have done the same," he said.

The others turned to look at him.

"If we'd had the support," Reginald went on, "we'd have done the same thing. I'd have pushed for it if there had been more than four of us. Barkley was an arrogant, evil prick. He didn't care for order. He wanted bloodshed. He fed on the panic that's been everywhere since the Ring of Fire, and he fanned the flames. He destroyed the Council. He was leading us to war. He'd have killed us all if he'd had his way."

With the mention of "the four of us," Reginald found himself thinking of Brian Nickerson and wondering if Brian had survived the sun when he'd stormed from the Council. Where had he gone? Had he gotten his family away, and had the Council pursued him? Reginald, Nikki, and Maurice had taken their families to Luxembourg. Where would Brian's family hide?

"But a *coup?*" said Maurice.

"Pretend you're on a ship," said Reginald. "The captain goes crazy and starts steering toward a waterfall or into a killer storm. Do you sit there and take it like a good soldier, knowing that he's doing the wrong thing, or do you rise up for the greater good, even if it means using your sword?"

All conversation had stopped. Someone had turned off the monitor showing the Council feed. Addled as his brain was, Reginald suddenly realized that he was giving a lecture. Even the EU Council had come to think of Reginald as the best strategic mind they had. The joke was on them, though, thought Reginald, because these days the most mental exercise he got was trying to tell Owen Wilson from Luke Wilson and deciding which of the killer asteroid movies from the 90s was the best.

"I don't know," said Karl, resuming his pacing. "I don't know."

"What if he doesn't give up the Council leadership?" said Nikki.

"Then Timken will rule instead of Barkley," said Mellus. "I don't really see the problem."

"He stormed in with *six hundred troops with deadly weapons*," said Nikki.

Reginald shrugged. Nikki saw the movement and looked over.

"This was how Maurice came to power," he said. "The only difference was that we actually *killed* Logan, whereas Timken has just taken Barkley into custody. If we'd been able, I'd have done it differently. I'd have killed Charles, too. I want him dead."

As soon as he'd said it, Reginald wanted to take it back. It sounded terrible, but it was true. He wanted Barkley dead. He wanted Walker dead. He'd been a punching bag for his entire human life, and he'd become even more of a punching bag once he'd become a vampire. *Fuck them.* Fuck *all* of them. Reginald was tired of being pushed around and pursued and persecuted and attacked and beaten up. He had the best mind of his species, and yet the first thing that most of the Nation looked at was his size. So fuck them. *Fuck. Them.*

"Me too," said Mellus.

Karl nodded. Then little by little, the assembly of vampires broke into groups. For now at least, the show was over.

Reginald felt relieved. He was tired. He needed to rest his mind and his eyes. He needed blood, too. He'd had too little of late, choosing instead to focus on comfort foods. He hated the taste of blood, but he'd have to suffer a few extra pints over the next few days in order to get himself back in shape. Like it or not, Karl and the others would be looking to Reginald more and more in the coming days and weeks.

As if reading Reginald's mind, Karl walked over and with a businesslike air said, "You will need to come to the summit in Paris. I can tell you are tired and drained, but you must go. Feed. Get ready. Especially after tonight, we will need you."

Reginald sighed. "Sure, Karl."

"And you too, Maurice. You are still the titular head in America."

"I'd planned on it," said Maurice. There was a heavy note in his voice. Maurice hated politics and he hated responsibility. He'd become Deacon because assassinating Logan had been the only way to escape, but he'd never wanted to be involved in the Council. He'd always been a rogue and a constant thorn in the Council's side.

"And me," said Nikki. She took Reginald's meaty forearm in her small, powerful hand. "Reginald and I are a package."

"Yeah," said Reginald, placing his other hand over Nikki's. He felt grateful. He needed Nikki, especially now. It wasn't every guy who was lucky enough to have a girl who could knock his face through a stone wall one minute and be his rock the next.

"Sure," said Karl, waving a hand theatrically to indicate that the matter was beneath him. "I like looking at your chest."

"Thanks," said Nikki. "I'll bring it with me."

NECESSARY

The summit was scheduled to occur in two days. Reginald predicted a clusterfuck.

According to Maurice and Karl, there had always been human authorities who knew that vampires existed. It wasn't a matter of cooperation so much as a matter of detente. The heads of the various Vampire Councils and the heads of their respective human regions kept in touch in the way that the United States and the Soviet Union had kept in touch at the height of the Cold War. They made a farce of diplomacy, but really all that mattered was that each considered the other to be a mortal threat. The vampires weren't going to stop feeding on humans, and humans who knew what they were facing weren't going to stop defending themselves and seeking out nests to exterminate. Both sides understood that skirmishes between their species were inevitable, so each made their peace with the existence of the other, accepted inevitable losses, and agreed that for the welfare of both sides, no official, large-scale action would be taken. As long as the Vampire Councils remained as hidden and low-key as possible, the human authorities wouldn't send the Anti-Vampire Taskforce's armies to dig them out while the sun was shining.

But over the past few months, the American Council's collapse had threatened that balance.

According to Karl, who'd been putting out diplomatic fires and smoothing ruffled feathers while Maurice was running for his life, American authorities were irate at the widespread killings being perpetrated by rogue vampires. They were threatening action. They already had AVT vampire hunters trained and ready, and were just looking for an excuse to set them loose. And so for months, Karl and the other Council leaders had been attempting to pacify the humans, assuring them that they were on top of "the American problem" — all the while knowing that if they *didn't* get on top of it, the AVT would soon engage worldwide. If that happened, vampires would find themselves facing a war on two fronts: from the angels on one side and from the humans on the other. And what made it worse was that it seemed impossible to serve both masters; the Ring of Fire suggested killing and turning, whereas peace with the humans forbade it. The balance was incredibly delicate.

"There was a time," said Karl as he used the Council's main computer to log in to the videoconferencing service, "when we didn't have such a nice balance with the humans. We've only 'agreed to disagree,' say, over the past two hundred and fifty years. Before that, it was the time of villagers and pitchforks and torches. Have you ever been chased by villagers with pitchforks and torches, Maurice?"

"Our whole nest was harassed by a bona-fide old-world village back before I moved to Virginia," said Maurice, nodding.

"Sometimes they chase me out of Burger King," said Reginald.

"I took a pitchfork through the head once," said Karl. "It was not pleasant. It was like he'd sharpened the points to be like daggers. A panicked and rather large woman swung a huge stone hammer and knocked me down, and her husband stood over me and drove the fork through my head — actually through my skull and brain — and into the ground. I guess he thought we were zombies. He couldn't pull it out, so he left it and marched toward the ruins of an old estate we'd holed up in. I stayed where I was until he was gone because I didn't want to take a chance that someone else might fork me or hit me again. I was young then, and not as strong. I was also not used to pain, and this pain was beyond the world. After he left, I freed myself and removed the thing. And when I made it back to the nest, they had burned it to cinders. Luckily it was evening. Villagers were idiots and always seemed to attack at night, so many of my fellows escaped. But five did not."

Even though Karl was telling what sounded to Reginald like a tragic story, he put his hands on his hips and looked wistfully into the distance, as if reliving a fond memory of the good old days. Reginald found himself expecting Karl to say something about how times were simpler then, or perhaps talk about how much you could buy with a dime. Or whatever currency they'd been using at the time, he mentally amended.

"Anyway," said Karl, "don't expect much of the friendly chatter at the summit. They will be extremely angry and they will make threats. It helps to think of them as villagers with pitchforks and torches, because that is essentially what they are underneath. It is our job to convince them that this was all Barkley's fault..."

"Which it wasn't," said Reginald.

"... and also that Timken represents a definite return to law and order."

"Which we don't know," Reginald added.

"Right. And we must not mention the elections. It is too uncertain. We must convince them that there is stability now, rather than more change."

"So we're presenting Timken as the leader in America, no question."

"Correct."

"And you're not worried that that gives him implied power."

"I cannot worry about that."

"And we're not mentioning the Ring of Fire."

"Correct," said Karl, now positioning the webcam. "Letting the humans know that many vampires believe we have a mandate from above to kill humans lest we be exterminated would be a *faux pas,* shall we say."

"We seem to be lying a lot in the spirit of cooperation," said Reginald.

"Don't feel guilty about it," said Maurice, his young-looking eyes locking onto Reginald's. "Rest assured, they will be lying to us."

Karl made a few final adjustments to the webcam and checked the settings in the videoconferencing software. Then he clicked a few places on the screen and they entered the conference, now able to see themselves in a small window in the corner of the screen. Their other party wasn't there yet. After a few moments, Reginald got tired of waiting and turned to Karl.

"Do you trust Timken?"

"He usually seems noble and he is very — how you say? — charismatic," said Karl.

That wasn't an answer. But before Reginald could repeat his question, a new, larger window appeared on the screen. The man in the window looked far less severe than he'd appeared during the coup. His blonde hair was combed neatly instead of mussed by a helmet and his narrow face, which had been serious and convicted, looked relaxed and handsome.

The man on the screen smiled. "Deacon Toussant!" he said, making a small bow toward Maurice. "It is nice to finally meet you. I am Nicholas Timken."

"Hello," said Maurice.

"And Karl, my old friend!"

"It is good to see you again, Nicholas," said Karl.

"And you," said Timken, leaning forward and looking directly into the camera rather than at the screen of his computer, "must be Reginald Baskin. It is a great pleasure to meet you."

" 'Sup," said Reginald.

"How are things abroad?" said Timken. "Will I see you at Oktoberfest, Karl?"

"Always a good time, Nicholas."

"Well," he said, "let's talk. I imagine you are curious about what happened yesterday."

"Slightly," said Karl.

"I regret that I had to take matters into my own hands. I also regret the fatalities. That was not intended. My men were to engage only if absolutely necessary, but a few in the crowd unfortunately made it necessary."

"I'm curious about the weapons they used," said Karl. "What are they, Nicholas?"

"They have an official name, but I call them Boom Sticks. Do you know those things doctors sometimes use to give injections without using a needle? Where they basically spray whatever it is through the skin? These work the same basic way, except that they're far, far more powerful."

"Powerful enough to go through clothes. Through skin and bone."

Timken tapped his chest and there was a metallic sound indicating that he wore something under his loose shirt. "Only reinforced armor will stop it."

"Where did such weapons come from?" Karl asked.

"I had them developed. They're state of the art." He smiled with self-satisfaction.

Karl's eyes narrowed. "They seem expensive. And lethal."

"Desperate times and deep pockets," said Timken, chuckling. "Besides, this is America, baby. Little old ladies carry grenades in their purses here."

Karl's lower jaw rocked below his upper jaw. His eyes were still serious, still penetrating the image on the screen.

"Look," said Timken, taking a breath. "I'll be straight with you. I started developing these right after the Ring of Fire. I thought there might be chaos. I wanted to be prepared. My company has provided me with a substantial amount of spendable funds, so I built a shelter and I purchased supplies. But swords and stakes and even wooden or silver bullets simply wouldn't be effective enough if there were riots. I wanted to defend myself. I was scared, to tell you the truth. And so when Barkley started calling the shots and things slowly went to shit in the streets, I found myself with a lot of supplies and a bunch of like-minded survivalist friends, and I saw a mission that needed to be undertaken. And you, Deacon —" His eyes moved to Maurice's side of the screen. "— were being persecuted and unable to command the armies we had, which shamefully abandoned their posts and went rogue. You couldn't protect the Nation, and I could. I tried peaceful means first; I really did. Karl *knows* I did. But they wouldn't listen, and things got worse and worse, and eventually it was down to a choice between overthrow and armageddon. So I got my friends together, and we took up weapons, and we did what was necessary."

"You called yourself an army."

Timken made a dismissive gesture. "Oh, you know how fighters are. They enjoy a label that gives them a sense of unity."

Karl's lower jaw continued to work. He chewed the inside of his cheek. Maurice and Reginald said nothing. They were there as observers, not truly participants. This was Karl's dance.

"All right, Nicholas. So what is next?"

"Elections, like I promised. I seized power because it was in the wrong hands, not because I wanted it for myself. I am a steward of this government's authority, nothing else." He opened his hands to show that he was merely a servant, there to do his duty to his species and his country. "The machinery is already in place, but I will make it better, and I'll open it to all the scrutiny it can take so that everyone can see that it's fair. The vampires of this country will vote in a free, open election, via Fangbook. We will elect a leader. We will restore order — not in the old,

Logan-type image, but in the image of the American government."

"Are you sure that's a good idea?" said Reginald.

Reginald said it as a joke, but Timken gave him a look. "Hey, love it or leave it," he said.

"And you will be a candidate?" said Karl.

"If the people want me. But so will you, Maurice, if you want to be. You are still the rightful authority, as far as I'm concerned."

Reginald looked at Maurice. Even if he wanted to rule the Council again, there was absolutely no chance he could win a free election. Maurice was one of the most loathed vampires on the planet. His views on inclusion of "sub-standard" vampires like Reginald and his other conservative, borderline reactionary views set him well outside of the comfort zones of the young US vampire population.

"No thanks," said Maurice.

"Then whoever," said Timken. "The more, the merrier. Anyone who wants to be on the ballot may be on it, and we'll let the people decide. We can guarantee a fair election. The Fang-book voting algorithm is unhackable — even by you, Mr. Baskin." The *you-sly-dog* expression that Timken gave Reginald left no question; he knew that Reginald had hacked the "unhackable" master algorithm that used to dictate the movements of the Vampire Council, back before it had plunked itself down in the basement of the Asbury Club and decided to make itself comfortable.

Karl nodded.

"Can you attend the summit in Paris in two days' time?" Karl asked.

"I can't leave. You must understand that."

"Of course," said Karl, nodding. He didn't want Timken to attend and knew he wouldn't be able to, but diplomacy said that he had to make the gesture.

"I could maybe attend like this," said Timken, pointing at his webcam. The gesture was boyish and playful.

"Perhaps it's best if we vouch for you," said Karl. "So that we can tell them our own version of events."

Timken nodded, understanding the need for subterfuge. From what Karl had told them earlier, Timken wasn't a diplomat, but he knew how the game was played — and when he should leave that game-playing to the people who knew how to play it best.

"I'm not exactly a summit kind of a guy anyway," said Timken, smiling. His smile was as large and handsome as Walker's, but not as insulting. It was welcoming and warm.

"Hmm," said Karl.

"Oktoberfest is more my speed."

Karl nodded.

"Eh, Karl?" said Timken. Big grin.

"Indeed."

"But you'll tell them that I'm here when the world needs me. That I'm keeping the Council warm for the next comer, and that in the meantime, our Nation will be ruled by order, not chaos."

"I will," said Karl. "Goodbye, Nicholas." He gave a small nod.

"Cheers," said Timken. Then he leaned forward and jabbed at something with his finger, and his window on the screen disappeared.

Karl exited the software, turned off the webcam, and stood. He stretched his back, putting a hand on his hips and arching his spine.

"He seems nice," said Reginald.

"Hmm."

"You don't think so?" said Reginald.

"Karl doesn't trust anyone," said Maurice.

"Hmm," said Karl.

TGV

Two days later, Reginald, Maurice, Nikki, and Karl left the Chateau and walked to the small Differdange train stop. The sun had almost set but was still up, low in the sky. That scared the bejesus out of Reginald and Nikki. Maurice, who'd often run to and from work just after sunrise using clothing and sometimes an umbrella to shield himself, was more sanguine. The day was overcast and the sun would set very soon, and they'd all worn special ultraviolet-repelling hoodies and gloves provided by a vampire tailor who shared shop space with a local human tailor. The hoods were very deep and Maurice assured them that as long as they stayed away from windows and remained covered, they'd be fine.

"Don't be wimps," Karl said to Nikki and Reginald. "I'm a thousand years older than you and would fry faster than you, but there is a direct TGV from Luxembourg to Paris at seven and I am sure as *scheiße* not taking a slow train because you are afraid of a sunburn."

So, duly bundled, the four vampires made their way to the train stop. Maurice and Karl walked confidently through the overcast day in their garb while Nikki and Reginald sprinted from faint shadow to faint shadow. Nikki could hide in the shadows of lampposts. Reginald couldn't hide in the shadows of anything other than buildings. He also couldn't sprint well and kept losing time when he collapsed or ran into startled pedestrians. Karl and Maurice arrived at the stop well before Reginald and Nikki, who crept up the stairs like spies and then crouched in a bush.

For Reginald, it was the furthest he'd been from the Chateau since they'd arrived in Europe three months earlier. He'd ventured to the Starbucks to use the Wi-Fi to download his movies (the Chateau's internet was pay-by-usage; the first bill after Reginald arrived had sent Karl into a rage) and to all of the local eateries that were still open after dark, which was most of them. The only restaurants he hadn't visited were the two health food restaurants. Nikki tried to get him to go to one of these on a date (she still liked carrot juice for some reason), but Reginald had said, "Why bother, I'm already dead." That had resulted in a fight. Nikki had gone back to the Chateau in a huff and Reginald had gone back a half hour later with three dozen donuts. He'd eaten eighteen immediately, then spent the rest of the evening complaining that he'd forgotten to get any with grape jelly inside. When Nikki protested, Reginald had told her that she'd *just* been trying to get him to eat healthier, and that grapes were a fruit. She'd tried to give him a glass of blood from the fridge. He'd refused. Knowing he was starving for the one thing a vampire needed, she then stirred blood into a cup of coffee so that Reginald could dunk his donut in it. Reginald "accidentally" spilled the blood coffee, then ran to Starbucks for a venti caramel mocha with whipped cream to replace it. He'd spent that day sleeping on a couch in one of the meeting rooms instead of in his bed with Nikki.

Now, out in the setting sun, it made him nervous to be so far from his comfort zone. The Chateau had become his world. The real world — the one outside — offered nothing but adversity and pain.

Once in Luxembourg City, they transferred to the TGV and

closed their blinds. Nikki and Maurice tried to sleep. Reginald found the snack stand and bought Doritos.

Shortly after leaving the station, night on the high-speed train blessedly fell. All four vampires stripped off their extra UV-proof gear and stowed it in their luggage with a sigh. Only after the mortal danger of the sun was safely below the horizon did everyone feel comfortable enough to settle in, so after tucking her hoodie away, Nikki pulled out her book and began reading slowly, at a languishing human pace. The cover showed a grizzled cowboy riding a unicorn and firing a gun in a puff of pink smoke.

"That looks like the stupidest book ever," said Reginald, who was agitated from the day's events and felt like picking a fight.

"It is. But it's better than yours," said Nikki.

Reginald, who liked reading when he throttled down his speed and took his time, had forgotten to bring a book. So, in order to not lose the argument, he pulled a Swiss home decor magazine from the rack and pretended to be enthralled by it. But after ten minutes, he sighed, conceded defeat, and put it back. Then he returned to his seat, opened the blind, and stared out the window into the dark French night.

Darkness had completely fallen outside. Even the light of the moon left little for the human passengers to see, but Reginald, with his vampire eyes, was able to see everything that they were passing. The train zipped along at 320 kph (Nikki, with her allergic reaction to the metric system, had asked for the mph conversion and Reginald had refused on principle) so everything next to the train was blurred, but farther out, he could see barns and fences and a few animals that had been left out late.

Trees. Sheds. Houses. Roads.

Reginald thought of how far he was from home — his *real* home, back in the States — and wondered if he'd ever see it again. He wondered if his house had been ransacked by Charles and his minions. He wondered if his old company had been able to move on and stay in business after the murders, and if it had been a second set of policemen (Reginald himself had glamoured the first set) who had first found the blood and carnage or if it had been an office worker who'd made that grizzly discovery. It might even have been a custodian. Reginald could imagine the custodian arriving, taking one look around at the blood-covered walls and the body parts, and then rolling his eyes and complaining that white-collar people were total slobs. Berger was dead. Most of the sales staff was dead — except for Walker, who had been responsible for at least a handful of the deaths himself. Most of accounting was dead. Who would run the place? Who would ever want to work in that building again, assuming they could get all of the blood out of the carpet?

Reginald watched France scream by the window.

He missed his couch. He missed his television. He missed sitting around doing nothing because it was all there was to life, as opposed to the way he'd been sitting around doing nothing recently in order to avoid reality. He missed being around humans, who were just as evil as vampires but who he could at least take comfort in knowing would die someday. He missed being a worthless fat guy, instead of the most important fat guy in the world. He missed the days when nobody expected anything of him.

He missed Claire.

He'd tried to call her before they'd left. He'd called late enough that she should have been home from school, but Reginald didn't know how normal Claire's life was these days. Her old routine was to attend school during normal hours, then to go to an afterschool program at a church down the street until late, because her mother worked late. But then her mother's schedule had changed, and Claire had gone to the church less often. That had been back before Victoria had been attacked by vampires and had become a kind of invalid. So was Claire still going to the afterschool program? Was she even still going to *school?* She and Victoria might have bunkered down, now only leaving the house for groceries during the brightest of afternoons. Given the increased frequency of vampire attacks — particularly in run-down neighborhoods like Claire's — Reginald sort of doubted the schools were paying much attention to who attended and who didn't anyway. Roll call these days probably accepted replies of, "Oh, he's dead" as normal. Principals these days probably sat in their offices with shotguns, unshaven and nursing a cup of brandy-spiked coffee, unsure what monsters they should be afraid of. Life was no longer what it used to be.

When Reginald had tried to call, the phone had rung and rung. Claire's family didn't own a cell phone; their phone system consisted of an ivory cordless and a similarly ivory wall unit with a cord so stretched out that it brushed the floor. They did have an answering machine. For the longest time, the voice on the machine was Victoria, but a week ago it had changed, and now it was Claire. Reginald wasn't sure how to feel about that. It meant that Claire was at least alive, and the fact that she'd thought to do something as trivial as re-record the answering machine message said several encouraging things in itself. Reginald sometimes called just to listen to the message, just to hear that ten-second snippet. He found himself trying to read her entire life from that brief segment of recorded voice. Didn't she sound more mature? Didn't she sound almost happy, or at least chipper? That was good, right? The message didn't sound defeated or beaten up. He listened to it the way the CIA watched video messages from terrorists. *Does the tone of this message sound like a person whose mother died recently?* he asked himself. He decided that it didn't, aware of just how ridiculous his assumption was. Still, he listened and he decided — if only to keep himself sane — that Claire was fine and that Victoria had hung on as well. She'd been not much more than a drained and bloody rag the last time Reginald had seen her in the alleyway, so it was good to hear — to believe — that she was okay.

Hi, you've reached the Hutchins Household.

And Reginald thought, *It's good to hear that she's healthy.*

We're not able to answer the phone right now...

And Reginald thought, *It sounds like she understands that Nikki, Maurice and I can't help what we are.*

... but if you leave us a message...

And Reginald thought, *Her mother is doing better and she's happy!*

... we'll call you back as soon as we can.

And Reginald had left a message, the same as he had many other times: *This is Uncle Reginald. I just wanted to check on you. I'd love to catch up. Here's how you can call me for free, or I'm always on Skype.*

Click.

And still Claire hadn't called, but it was okay. Reginald could hear the lack of anger in her answering machine message and knew that everything was going to be okay.

Nikki didn't ask Reginald about Claire anymore. At first, she'd been as neurotic as Reginald had. They'd tried to pick Claire up before fleeing to Europe, but she hadn't come out of her house. They'd tried to call — frequently at first, then less and less often as time went on. Reginald still called several times a week, but when the answering machine message changed, Nikki stopped trying. To Reginald, the message change meant that Claire was alive and well. To Nikki, it meant that Claire had gotten every one of their messages and was choosing to ignore them.

Outside the window, the world whipped by. Reginald wondered if Maurice could run as fast as this train. He decided that the answer was yes, but also decided that even Maurice, who was currently asleep two seats down, appreciated the value of sitting back and letting someone else do the work for a change.

With that thought, before he could stop it, Reginald's thoughts flitted into Maurice's mind. Maurice's eyelid fluttered, and Reginald forced himself to pull back. Maurice and Reginald, as maker and progeny, would always share the bond of blood. But during their escape from the Council, Reginald had discovered that not only could he read vampires he was related to, but that he could, to some degree, control them as well. Afterward, when Reginald told Nikki and Maurice that he had been sending them what they'd thought were their own inspirations to move, both had been shocked. Maurice had been paranoid ever since. Out of respect, Reginald had tried to stay out of his mind, but it wasn't easy. They were like the closest of brothers. When Maurice was hungry, Reginald felt it. When Maurice was happy, Reginald's mood lifted. Secrets were hard to keep. And lately, something else had started to happen, something he hadn't shared with Maurice. He could now sometimes see pictures from Maurice's mind. He could almost see through Maurice's eyes. It was no longer just about telepathy and control. The feeling was closer to slipping on a Maurice suit — or would be, if Reginald indulged it, which he didn't.

But when he did — when he slipped into Maurice's blood, before he caught himself — he could get a sense of Maurice's entire bloodline. There were amazing and dreadful vampires in Maurice's family history. Maurice had always said that it was common to feel a connection (Nikki still sometimes dealt with out-of-control thirst that Maurice attributed to ties along her bloodline; she was, in essence, feeling the emotions of others) but this was different. It was like logging in to a network. Once he'd tuned in to Maurice, he gained access to those others. And he suspected — but had never tested — that if he were to step fully into Maurice's mind, he'd feel the relations closest to Maurice as being as mentally close as Maurice himself felt them. And then Reginald might be able to step into *their* minds from Maurice's, and thus hopscotch up and down vast bloodlines, seeing the thoughts and sights of vampires worlds distant without ever leaving his chair. He could transcend great distances. He might even be able to experience movement back and forth through time.

Reginald looked one seat closer, at Nikki. Her book was open on her lap, but her eyes were closed. She really was beautiful. He felt a sudden sense of attraction, looking at her now, that he realized he may never have fully felt before. He'd been traumatized by life and by Walker and by his newfound vampirism when they'd met. Shortly thereafter, he'd been on trial for his life. Nikki had come with him when the Balestro and Ring of Fire affairs had occurred, and they'd co-habitated on and off throughout the disintegration of the Vampire Nation and the crumbling of the Council. Life since becoming a vampire had, for Reginald, been one long string of perilous situations, most of which made him feel inadequate and unprepared. Nikki had been by his side the whole time, but there had always been an emotional wall between them — despair in the face of defeat, sarcasm in the face of success. Had he ever had the quintessentially *human* experience of looking at Nikki and simply being attracted to her... of wanting her in a way that was divorced from the simple, factual truth of her availability at his side? He wasn't sure. Guys like Reginald didn't look at women like Nikki and hope to be with them. They *wanted* women like Nikki, sure — but *hope?* Hope implied that trying might lead to success. Hope was a light at the end of the tunnel. But it hadn't been that way with Nikki. She'd simply been there by his side from the beginning, before he'd had a chance to want or to hope. That easiness had leapfrogged him right past the stage of pining. Really, he thought now, it had kept him from appreciating her. It had kept him from being as aghast as he should be that she was with him at all.

Because he was her maker, he could see in Nikki's mind, too.

Sitting in the train, he did.

Reginald closed his eyes. He felt the vibration of the train underneath him. His head thrummed against the headrest. The world became a dull red as his eyes saw the insides of his eyelids in the train's interior lights, but then he gave a push and it was as if someone had turned off the lights. The vibration was gone, too. Reginald felt himself floating down a tunnel. Only he wasn't Reginald; he was Reginald's spirit, or ghost, or consciousness. He didn't feel clumsy or awkward.

He found Nikki, felt her blood. It wasn't like seeing her, but he *could* see; there was a green and sun-lit landscape he'd encountered before when his mind had touched Nikki — something she knew, or missed, or that represented a world she'd never see again in reality now that she'd given herself to the night.

He could feel himself slipping into her, putting her on like a glove. But it wasn't an intrusion; she felt his presence and he felt her sensing his presence, and she invited him in. The morose self-pity of the past months had fallen away. Reginald felt light. Something about looking over at her with his eyes open; something in his head had clicked and he'd realized who he was and where he was without pondering the baggage of how he'd gotten here. Right now, he was Reginald Baskin; he was a vampire; he was perhaps the most mentally advanced vampire in centuries and very important to the species's survival; he had a mission that he could handle; he was with a beautiful young vampire who would be beautiful forever.

Nikki's thoughts colored yellow, then pink. The pink surrounded him like a caress. He felt a smile — though in here, neither of them had lips. He felt a sense of pleasure. He wasn't sure if it was his own. He sensed a halfhearted rebuke, a playful chastising of Reginald's mind for invading hers. Then her thoughts wrapped him and he felt her all around him. A series of rebus images appeared in front of him, each only for a fraction of a second, speeding at him and each leaving a mental imprint. He was seeing her mood, her impressions, her mental landscape, her feelings and desires: blood, a flower opening in a time-lapse video, lips on the skin of a long, soft neck, fangs descending, a deep, warm breath, her lips, a hand on a naked breast, a trickle of blood welling in the hollow beneath a clavicle, a tongue, an embrace. Reginald felt his own thoughts and images flowing out into the pool of hers, swirling and mixing. The thoughts touched and combined, shifted, changed shape. The blood became his blood. Became her blood. The warm breath was hers, on his neck. The hand was his and the naked breast was hers.

Then, in the corner of their shared thoughtscape, the warm pink feeling darkened. Reginald felt it happen, raised a metaphorical head to look. Nikki sensed it, but he could tell that she couldn't see it as he could; she was sensing *his* sensation of whatever it was. But whatever it was, it was growing. The cloud of eroticism began to disperse; mental Reginald sat up. Mental Nikki pulled the sheets over her metaphorical bodiless body and mentally asked him what was wrong. The corner became less and less pink, more and more black. It became like a peephole. Reginald saw a dark night through someone else's eyes. Felt gravel crunch under someone else's feet. Felt cool air on someone else's skin.

Nikki's thoughts lost their pink color, became the darker maroon color of blood. Somewhere there was a heartbeat, always still strange to him in a vampire's mind or chest. He felt her thoughts quicken, somehow disturbed by what Reginald sensed, not because she could see it but because she knew Reginald could.

Reginald stepped more fully into the black peephole, feeling Nikki recede to a maroon halo of feeling behind him. It was like she was watching over his shoulder now. He could feel the other person's

(vampire's)

feet crunch on the rock below. It was small rock, like gravel. The picture was becoming clearer and clearer, as if he were coming more fully within its broadcast range. He felt the breeze more acutely. He saw objects around him in the darkness. A barn that was probably bright white during the day now visible as a shadow to his left. Fences. Fields. Sheds. He felt the body he was in lean forward, as if preparing to take a tackle. Below his feet he felt the gravel move as the body shifted. His peripheral vision showed him horizontal, parallel slats of wood among the gravel.

And long, smooth rails of metal. Vibration was coming up this other's legs from below. And a light ahead, rapidly approaching.

Closer.

Closer.

A whistle. The sound of onrushing doom.

Inside the train, Reginald's eyes snapped open to find that he was staring directly into Nikki's eyes, wide awake and terrified. He reached over to Maurice to shake him, to warn him, but it was too late.

SWEEPERS

The sound of the collision and derailment was like the world ending. There was a titanic booming noise, like a bomb, and Reginald felt himself thrown forward as the front of their car crumpled and bent like a tin can. Seats sheared away as roof met floor. Glass shattered and peppered the air. He struck something hard and felt his right arm crushed and pulled off; a bulkhead (some massive piece of metal, anyway) screamed toward and smashed his face and then for a while, everything was black while his eyes healed. Gravity shifted; he felt himself alternately flying, floating, being thrown forward and up, whipping toward the back of the car as, presumably, the whole thing spun end for end.

He didn't think to slow his mind (the time-stopping trick, if he could manage it in his rusty state) to analyze the minutia of the experience. This was something he wanted to end as fast as possible. His mind called out to Nikki and Maurice and even Karl, who he'd never before been able to feel. He couldn't find them, but he could hear screaming, and he felt relatively sure that at least some of it was in his head — which, as long as it didn't cut off suddenly, was actually a good thing because it meant that they were alive. There were many, many human noises. Most were like thumps of meat being struck with a hammer. He heard yells and panicked screams. There was an odd sensation of hundreds of people holding their breath, unable to breathe as the cars upended and tumbled. As the cars landed and rolled and he fell up and down and then up again, many of the human screams ended and new ones began, but even those didn't last for long before going silent. There was more booming, more crunching of metal. The car was jerked forward suddenly, everything in it slamming into what was barely still a rear wall. Everything had become sharp protrusions and crushing vises. His vision came and went.

Maybe four seconds had passed. And then, for a while, blessedly, there was nothing.

———

REGINALD AWOKE to find his head clear but everything below his chest in agony. Apparently the trick his body sometimes had of shutting off pain in perilous situations was also rusty, because right now everything hurt. He raised his head, which was whole and without a scratch on it, and looked down to see that he had a gigantic metal fin protruding from his torso. The car had folded more or less in half and had split along the crease, creating a forest of sharp protrusions. Reginald seemed to have landed on one of those protrusions. He looked toward his legs and found them whole but half naked. There was a huge pile of gray ash beside the left leg with fabric lying on top of it that looked like his pants, and Reginald wondered if, while he'd been blacked out, he'd lost a leg and re-grown it.

There was an itch in his mind. Something he couldn't quite put a finger on. Something was wrong that had nothing to do with the actual crash itself. He needed to get off this fin so that he could escape.

Reginald shifted his weight and found that the pain, as he

tried to move, was beyond the world. It would be better to just stay where he was, he decided.

No. Move.

There was urgency behind that thought, but things were still too foggy. All that mattered was getting out.

He tried to put his hands under himself and push, but one of his arms refused to come along. He looked over and saw that the arm on one side was crushed under what seemed to be a luggage compartment. There was still luggage inside. He could see a Samsonite suitcase that had survived just fine, just as Samsonite promised. There was an ugly bag near it that looked as if it were made out of carpet, and this one hadn't fared as well. Reginald could make out a wallet, a loose drugstore card, an annihilated cell phone, and a danish wrapped in cellophane. For one comic-horrible moment, Reginald imagined himself squirming over and, without use of his arms, sucking down the danish like Popeye did with spinach whenever he got into a jam. His belly would bulge and color would return to his limbs and he'd then split the car in half with his corpulence, freeing them all.

Hurry.

And that thought was insistent, but what was becoming more insistent — even more than the giant metal fin that had almost bisected him — was finding the others. They had to be here. They couldn't have been impaled by wood, so as long as they'd managed to avoid a direct beheading, Nikki, Maurice, and Karl would still be alive, probably trapped like he was. And why not? Reginald could still hear humans making noises. Plenty of them, frail as they were, seemed to have survived. For now, anyway.

Nikki! he thought.

He reached out his mind. They hadn't quite gotten the hang of true telepathy, as Nikki's vampire enhancements hadn't gifted her mind as strongly as they'd gifted his. But if he concentrated, he could always find her. And then, after a moment, he did. He slipped inside of her head, knowing that it was a violation but deciding that the situation excused it. He saw a crushed leg, Nikki's own. She was working herself free. Then he reached out for Maurice and found him, too. Maurice was already free, already searching. But he wasn't searching openly, and that gave Reginald pause. He was hiding behind felled seats, moving from place to place warily, as if playing a war game. Maurice wasn't looking for Reginald or Nikki. He could feel that Reginald and Nikki had survived. Instead, he was looking for Karl.

Reginald looked at his pinned arm. Just thinking about it hurt. He wondered why his panic response wasn't kicking in. Then, in a regression into Eeyore self-loathing, he decided that it was because he was Reginald and that Reginald's body had always betrayed him.

He wasn't going to be able to pull himself off of the metal fin without his arms. And he wasn't going to get his arm back without...

Ugh. He didn't want to think about it.

The arm wasn't hanging on by much. If he could sever it, it would regrow on the end of the stump and he'd be free.

He looked at the fin sticking through his middle.

Well, free-ish, anyway.

Reginald rolled away from the pinned, mostly severed arm in its pool of blood and pulp, then tried to use his weight to jerk it hard enough to snap it off. But every time he tried, the fin cut something in his torso and lit his mind up like fire. It would almost be easier if he *weren't* a vampire, if he *couldn't* heal. The fin hurt especially bad because he was cutting the same flesh open over and over again, causing fresh gluts of blood to roll out and down his shirt. And each time afterward, he healed everything except the part where the fin was, clamping him to it tightly.

The other problem was that most of his abdominal muscles had been severed. He couldn't sit up or roll well at all. Core musculature was mostly out of the picture.

Maybe he could *stand* off of the fin.

He bent his legs up, planted his feet, and pushed. But he didn't budge, and when he looked down, he realized why. His legs weren't bent up at all. His feet weren't planted at all. He tried to move his legs again, but they didn't move. Apparently his spine was also bisected.

Awesome.

He lifted his other hand, thinking that maybe his surprisingly strong fingers could peel the fin, or rip it off. But the hand flopped like a dead fish — wholly intact but with its tendons and supporting musculature severed, making it useless.

He was running out of options.

There's only one way to do this, and you know it, said a heckling voice in his head.

Reginald closed his eyes, took as deep of a breath as his lungs would allow, and leaned toward his crushed arm. He flicked out his fangs.

Then, making faces of revulsion, he went to work.

———

NIKKI FOUND him a few minutes later. She climbed a mountain of human gore and detached seats and arrived just as Reginald was heaving himself off of the giant metal fin using his newly grown arm.

"Thank God," she said. "You're alive."

Reginald spit, then wiped at his mouth with his sleeve.

"I just chewed my own fucking arm off," Reginald replied, making a disgusted face and indicating the pile of ash under the luggage compartment. Once the arm had collapsed to ash, the compartment laying on it had shifted, causing the cellophane-wrapped danish to tumble out. Reginald had taken it as a sign. He was unwrapping it now, preparing to devour it as if he had a grudge against it.

"Do you know where Maurice is?" she said.

"I could feel him around. He's free. Looking for Karl. I don't know where."

Reginald felt his strength — what he had of it — returning. The danish seemed to be helping. So it was like with Popeye.

"Your boobs are out," he said.

They were. So were Reginald's. If they'd been humans, they'd both be dead, but as vampires they'd been able to take the slashing abuse that their clothes couldn't, leaving them alive but exposed.

Nikki made a halfhearted attempt to pull her slashed bra over her breasts, then tugged at what had become a belly shirt. It didn't help. Reginald continued to stare, fully aware of how inappropriate it was under the circumstances.

"We derailed," she said.

"So you're saying this isn't the Avignon stop?"

Nikki's eyebrows furrowed. "We aren't anywhere near Avignon."

"Because *that's* what's important right now."

Nikki flicked her head around nervously. "Karl said earlier that there are several other vampire and human dignitaries on board. Very seriously doubting the humans survived. I guess this puts a crimp in the summit. Son of a bitch stroke of bad luck."

"It wasn't bad luck. We were deliberately derailed. I thought you knew that."

"How would I know that?"

Reginald thought of her wide, terrified eyes just before the crash.

"Never mind. We have to..."

But then he stopped, because there was a loud, rending noise below them.

Because of the way the car had bent, Nikki and Reginald were up on a peak in the middle of the car. Nikki had come through a hole in the next car and had climbed up, following a kind of homing radar that they shared. It was what Reginald was about to use to find Maurice and hopefully Karl when he'd heard the noise. Without the radar, Nikki wouldn't have easily seen him. He was above, in a fold. Most of the car's contents, including a handful of still-living humans, were lower down.

Reginald peeked around the edge of the luggage compartment that had trapped his arm. Nikki, her hand on his shoulder and her bare breasts pressed into his back, peered over his shoulder.

The rending noise had been a man in a vintage-looking black suit opening a hole in the side of the car with his hands, peeling the metal back like a can of sardines. He had a thick black goatee, large, severe eyebrows, and a shock of black hair that was sticking more or less straight up. He strolled through the hole he'd made and looked around as if inspecting racks of clothing at a department store.

Reginald could see a group of three humans (they looked like teenage tourists — European, judging by their clothes) look toward the man as he came in. They didn't seem to find it odd that he'd opened a hole in the car with his hands. All they cared was that he was here to rescue them.

A girl with long blonde hair who seemed to have only sustained a broken leg hobbled up and reached toward him and began speaking in French, all nonsense syllables amounting to *Help us* and *Save us* and *Please* and *Please*. Everything came out amongst pained sobs, her hair in her face, snot running down her upper lip.

The man in the black suit grabbed her by the throat in a movement that was too quick to see, then used both hands to hold her up to his mouth. There was a crunching sound and a scream, and then the vampire drank as the girl went limp. Her two companions began to scream and thrash, but they were both more injured than she was and could only crawl, and within moments he'd disposed of them, too.

Nikki's hand tightened on Reginald's shoulder. They both slunk back further, out of sight. Reginald could feel Nikki's breath on the back of his neck. Nikki might be able to take on the newcomer, but she'd have to stumble through the wreckage to get down to him, and that would give him time to turn and respond. Besides, Reginald could tell from her body language that she was too shocked to do anything. Plenty of vampires killed humans, of course, but Nikki had always been so careful to "sip and ship" — glamouring her victims and sending them along instead of letting them die. She'd always vowed, privately to Reginald, that she'd never forget that she herself had once *been* human, and that she'd once been frightened of the world's monsters, too.

The man in the black suit walked across the length of the train car, stepping over the three new bodies, wiping his mouth and goatee on a hanging blouse from someone's spilled suitcase. There was carnage everywhere. Too many dead humans to count. Too much twisted metal and broken luggage and detritus to believe. The man walked across the piles of bodies and wreckage, casually scanning the seats. As Nikki and Reginald watched, he found two more survivors and killed them using only his hands. He didn't bother to drink. Then he reached the end of the car and, finding the door jammed, kicked it hard enough to punch a hole in the metal. He widened the hole with his hands, stepped through, and was gone.

"What the hell was..."

But Reginald put his finger to his lips, his pulse quickening. His heartbeat was loud enough in his ears that he felt like it might give him away, and for the thousandth time, he wished that vampire lore had turned out to be true. He should be a beautiful, thin corpse by now, not a fat nervous wreck.

"*What?*"

Reginald tapped his finger more insistently against his lips, his eyes widening. It was the silent version of yelling at her to shut up, irritated that she hadn't taken the point the first time.

He pointed.

Two more black-clad vampires — a man and a woman — had

entered the car through the hole made by the first. A second man then climbed in from the outside through a shattered window — a shocking accomplishment, since the windows weren't made of glass. All three of the new vampires wore the same vintage black suit as the first man, but these three were being far more thorough than he had been. They were peering under every pile of debris, checking every seat. They were opening compartments and moving aside huge pieces of metal as if they weighed nothing. The first vampire had been a quick initial pass. This was the cleanup crew, here to make sure that nothing survived.

The first thought Reginald had about the crash that didn't involve pain and blood had been that this must be the work of vampire radicals — the kind that had stormed his old office and killed those inside because they were "only human." This was supposed to be about rebellion and panic and the preservation of the great vampire race... but that was *all* it was supposed to be. Kill some humans. Cause some chaos. Have some laughs. It wasn't supposed to be so methodical. So deliberate. So cold.

He watched the three vampires, all in suits that matched perfectly enough to be uniforms. He thought of the two-pass strategy — a blitzkrieg attack followed by a careful second sweep to finish any surviving enemies.

This is an extermination.

And here they were, hidden but in no position to fight. Reginald was useless even under the best of conditions, and right now he didn't even have his spooky pain invulnerability to give him a layer of protection. Nikki could fight, and in theory, Reginald could guide her as he had back in Columbus, and make her better. But he didn't trust himself. Everything had felt new again recently. His strategic mental muscles felt tired and rusty. He couldn't block pain. And worst: even if he *could* direct Nikki to dodge and weave and evade and kill as needed, they'd never make it down to where the vampires were without alerting them. And no matter how much he could slow things down and move Nikki like a puppet, that wouldn't change how prepared they'd be to take her on if she gave them enough time during her descent.

No, they were trapped. As long as they could hide in their nook they'd be safe, but what were the chances that they could stay hidden?

"Check under that pile," said the first man, who was as tall and thin as a scarecrow. He had an angular face and big, blue eyes.

"Don't tell me how to do my fucking job," said the woman. There were undertones in the way she said it, and Reginald suspected that the tall man had been nagging her for a while, probably pointing at every pile in every car they'd come through.

"Just do it. Nobody has found Stromm yet."

Nikki turned to Reginald and mouthed: *Karl.*

Reginald nodded.

"They won't," said the woman. "Jesus, this is stupid."

"It's not the main reason he did it, Wynona. Chances are that Stromm healed and ran. But would you like to be the one to tell him that Stromm *was* in fact here, pinned somewhere, and that we just *missed* him? So stop bitching and *check under that fucking pile.*"

The man pointed again and the woman glared at him. She was half his size, but that meant nothing. Maurice looked like a hollow-chested teenager, but at two thousand years old, few vampires could stand against him if they met on equal footing.

Finally, with a huff, the woman and the tall man broke their tableau. The woman blurred to the pile of debris. Reginald watched as she hunched over it and, with the air of a child having a tantrum, seized a collapsed bulkhead with one hand and pulled it upward so fast and so hard that it exploded through the top of the car, sending bits of new debris raining down. The impact jolted the entire compartment and the two other vampires fell to the ground, sprawling over the bodies of the French teenagers.

"Fucking *cunt!*" yelled the tall man, righting himself. He was across the car in a blur and had the woman by her black vintage lapels. Then they spun and he pushed her hard into the exposed metal wall of the car, denting it outward with a pop. "Do you think we have all the time in the world here? Do you think that there might not already be human authorities on their way? Are you trying to expose us?"

The woman, a small, wry smile on her face, nodded her head toward the place where the collapsed bulkhead had been laying.

"He's not under there," she said. Then she grabbed his crotch and began to rub.

The third vampire

(Claude)

was watching the fight / grope session. He rolled his eyes and said,

Knock it off, dammit.

"Knock it off, dammit."

The woman looked at the man, who was was built like a brick wall. His shoulders were so wide and his back so thick that he transformed his formal dress into an oddity. It was as if someone had dressed the Incredible Hulk in a suit just so that they could watch him rip the seams and burst out of it.

"You want some too, don't you, Claude?" She made a gripping, stroking motion in the air toward him.

The sooner we can finish the sweep, the sooner we can get out of here.

"The sooner we can finish the sweep, the sooner we can get out of here," he said.

Reginald realized he was hearing the big vampire in his head before the man spoke. He looked at Nikki and mouthed, *Can you hear that?*

Nikki: *What?*

Reginald enunciated more clearly, exaggerating the movement of his lips: *Can. You. Hear. That?*

Nikki, aloud, in a whisper: "What?"

The big man named Claude jerked his head upward at the sound. But that was okay, because Reginald had heard Nikki's voice twice — once in his own ears and once through Claude's. And with that, he knew what it all meant.

Claude was the vampire who'd stood on the tracks, who'd taken the collision and derailed the train. It was Claude whose eyes he'd seen through before. And because Reginald was sharing his thoughts, that meant that somehow, in some way, Reginald's blood was related to Claude's. And *that* meant that if he wanted to, Reginald could control him.

"There's someone up there," said the tall vampire. His big blue eyes looked up toward the fold in the car. And the tall vampire began to climb.

Climb, Reginald told Claude.

The big vampire began to climb up the nearly vertical seats in the folded section of the car.

I've got this, Reginald thought.

Claude climbed over while moving up, putting himself between the other vampire and Reginald. Then he put a hand out, placing it on the thin vampire's chest.

"I've got this," he said.

"I want a taste if there's anything human up there," said the tall vampire, smiling a humorless smile as his fangs popped out.

Keep searching.

"Keep searching," said Claude.

Now come up, Reginald commanded, *and look me in the eye.*

Claude's big face came into view in front of Nikki and Reginald. He had a square jaw and a massive scar curving from his forehead down to his neck — a souvenir he must have gotten before turning and would be stuck with it forever. Reginald found himself wondering with fascination how Claude, as a man, had gotten the scar and how the injury hadn't killed him. (Or, Reginald amended, maybe it *had* killed him.) His eyes were hazel. His face seemed almost friendly.

Reginald watched Claude's face, watched his own face through Claude's eyes.

There's nothing up here, Reginald thought at him.

"There's nothing up here," Claude shouted to the others.

Now go. You saw nobody.

Claude jumped down to the bottom of the car in one big leap, landing on what might have been a severed arm and faltering before righting himself. Then he moved on, toward the hole in the other end of the car.

The others followed him. A few moments later, they were gone and Reginald and Nikki were alone.

SNICK

Reginald and Nikki waited a few more minutes to make sure that no more vampires in black suits were coming through the car before moving. There was no rush. After the group of three had moved on, Reginald told Nikki that he'd been keeping tabs on Maurice,` and that Maurice had found Karl. He'd told Maurice, in the same way he'd Claude, to leave them and head back to the Chateau. There was no point in making a stand. Whatever group was clearing the train, they were organized and there were a lot of them. There would be no helping the humans, most of whom were dead already. Reginald and Nikki were safe, and they'd leave when the coast was clear. The best strategy would be to retreat and regroup, then compare notes.

"You told him all of that like... like an ESP message?" Nikki asked. They were walking across a damp French field, and she was wearing a long night shirt that had a giant picture of Alfred E. Newman on it above the laconically stenciled legend *J'en ai rien à foutre.* Before they'd left the wreckage of the TGV and set out on foot, Nikki had pulled the shirt from someone's luggage to hide her upper-body nakedness. Reginald had found a robe to hide his own, but he did so with the air of protecting onlookers rather than depriving them, which was what Nikki was doing.

"I pretty much just told him to leave," Reginald admitted. The truth was too complicated to explain. It was as if he'd planted a subconscious suggestion. Maurice would think that it had been his idea. Reginald would, once they returned, feel honor-bound to explain that he had sent Maurice the imperative, and Maurice would be furious because he felt that Reginald manipulating him was a violation, which of course it was. But Reginald would take Maurice's fury over his death, and that's what would have happened had Maurice felt compelled to search until he found them.

"And that other one. That big guy? When he started climbing up, I thought we were screwed. But you...?" She raised her eyebrows. It was dark, but there was a moon, and Reginald saw her gesture just fine.

"Yeah. Apparently he and I... and therefore he and you... are related."

"Related?"

"Well, we're all related, ultimately," said Reginald. "Especially if the Cain legend is true. But I noticed I could hear his thoughts. It was his eyes I saw through before the derailment."

Nikki was quiet for a few seconds. The only sounds were the squishing of their shoes in the soft ground.

"You can glamour vampires," she said finally.

"I seem to be able to influence blood that's close to mine," he said.

"That's splitting hairs."

"Maybe. But I have to remind myself, ever since that morning we got out of The Asbury, that hearing other vampires' thoughts is trespassing. It doesn't feel that way, though. It feels like I'm talking to my own blood. That's the way it seems to me, like I'm telling my own arm to do something, or seeing something through my own eyes. Especially when it happens with you and Maurice.

He made me and I made you. He's forever in me and I'm forever in you."

Nikki sniggered.

"Grow up."

"I'm not being immature," she said. "I'm being horny."

Reginald stopped. His feet squished in mud. In the distance, the wreck of the TGV was still visible. Helicopters and rescue squads had arrived and the entire site was awash in light. The rescuers would find nothing but hamburger and ash, and then higher authorities would intervene and the official version would report that it had been a freak accident that had killed one hundred percent of its passengers. Perhaps a cow had broken through the fence and stumbled onto the track.

"How can you be horny?" he said.

Reginald was wearing a backpack. He'd found it just outside the train and had filled it with candy bars and snack foods a few cars further down, where they'd discovered an ejected snack cart. In his hand and in his cheeks was a Chunky bar.

"How can *you* be hungry?" she countered.

"It's my coping mechanism," he said.

Nikki gave him a small shrug.

Reginald nodded, conceding a point made, and resumed walking.

A half hour later, they found a country road and waited for a car to pass. Eventually one did, but it refused to stop when they waved at it. A few minutes later, another car approached, and again they waved, and again the car drove on. Nikki was more aggressive when the next pair of headlights appeared, standing halfway into the lane. The car swerved wide and kept going.

So as the next car approached, Reginald laid down in the middle of the road. Nikki danced around above him, waving and trying to look like the distraught relative of an unfortunate hit-and-run. This time the car did stop, but not in time. The driver was talking on a cell phone and laid on the brakes just ten feet from Reginald. Nikki dove out of the way and Reginald, seeing the writing on the wall, tried to stand. But a half-second later, the car ran him over and became briefly airborne as if it had struck a giant speed bump.

Reginald made a formidable obstacle. The car flew fifteen feet and barrel-rolled onto its side before coming to a stop amidst much sparking and grinding of metal. Reginald felt his face crushed by the car's left front tire and felt his genitals pulverized by the left rear. What the other tires did was irrelevant by comparison; before it rolled, the car dragged him several dozen feet and rubbed him against the road like cheese across a cheese grater.

Cracking his neck, Reginald stood. His wounds healed, leaving his clothing tattered and shredded for the second time in two hours. The back was especially bad. Nikki actually laughed when he said his back was cold, then reported that everything was visible from his shoulders to his ass to his heels.

Reginald, fifty percent naked, walked over to the car. It was one of those tiny, boxy European jobs. The driver was a young man with long, stringy blonde hair. He was wearing a giant rainbow Rastafarian hat over his fried mane. The car reeked of marijuana through its broken windows.

Nikki was looking down into the car, her back arched, her palms on her knees. The car's airbag had gone off and the kid had been wearing his seatbelt. Good for him.

The kid groaned. Then he looked up.

"My bad," said Reginald. "I didn't think you'd hit me."

"Did I hit you, dude?" the kid croaked. He sounded American. He looked at the two vampires, seemingly trying to decide if he was dreaming.

"Yeah. I don't recommend it."

"Dude, I'm sorry," he said. "That's *my* bad."

"It's cool, dude."

"Dude."

Nikki looked from the kid to Reginald and rolled her eyes.

The kid, sideways in the car with the airbag deflating in his face, covered in cubes of safety glass, his scalp bleeding, a joint actually still in the corner of his mouth, held up a fist.

"Respect bump," he said.

Reginald bumped his fist.

Nikki reached down and began prodding at the kid, pushing him randomly. The touch made him laugh as if he were ticklish or possibly just really high. Like a pothead doughboy.

"Are you hurt?"

"I think I'm cool."

"Hang on."

Nikki walked to the rear of the car and picked it up by its trunk. Then she rotated it and set it back down on its tires. None were flat.

"Dude," said the kid. "Did you just pick up my car?"

Nikki looked at Reginald. Reginald stepped forward and prepared to glamour the kid, but then the kid in the car said, "Are you vampires, dude?"

Reginald shrugged at Nikki. Then he looked through the car's window and said, "Yeah."

Nikki made violent gestures at Reginald.

"That's cool," said the kid, digging a lighter from his pocket to re-light the joint. "You want a ride?"

So they rode. The kid's name turned out to be Snick, which Reginald decided might not be his birth name. He drove the entire way while toking up and singing Credence Clearwater Revival songs, then dropped them off at a train station. Reginald thanked him for the ride. Snick thanked them for not biting him and then offered up another fist bump. Reginald gave it. Nikki rolled her eyes.

Moving from rail to rail and glamouring whoever they needed in order to secure free passage, they made their way back to Differdange, finally stumbling through the door to the giant stone staircase just before sunrise. They found Maurice waiting in the cathedral room, pretending to read. When Maurice saw them, Reginald immediately found himself squeezed in a bone-crushing hug. Maurice picked them both up off of the floor. Reginald heard a rib crack, then and asked Maurice to put them down.

"You took the long way, I take it?" he said.

"We walked," said Reginald.

He didn't offer more. He caught a glimpse of Maurice's thoughts and knew that he'd followed the tracks all the way back to Rheims, where he'd caught a local train to take him the rest of the way. Reginald and Nikki hadn't done the same. Reginald couldn't run that far that fast, but Nikki could, even with Reginald on her back — but Reginald had wanted to spend time putting one foot in front of the other, letting his mind's wheels turn. He was still coming to rediscover his own head. He had to find the mental groove that had gotten so rusty over the past few months.

Maurice stepped back and cocked his hands on his narrow hips. His left hand brushed the hilt of his sword, which was safely back in its scabbard after being broken during their escape from the Asbury club. He'd had it repaired by a metalsmith soon after arriving, and Reginald had subsequently expressed astonishment that metalsmiths still existed.

"Well," said Maurice.

"The derailment was intentional," said Reginald.

"Yes."

"And I'm related to the vampire who did it."

Maurice nodded, his eyes finding the corner of the room. He sighed.

"Yes. I saw him. His name is Claude Toussant. He's my brother. My literal big brother. We were turned together, but haven't spoken for hundreds of years. I wanted to say hello using my teeth when I saw him on the train, but he was with a group. It just seemed much smarter to head back and meet you back here."

Reginald said nothing. He could tell Maurice later about the impulse he'd delivered into his mind. This didn't feel like the time.

Maurice sat heavily in an overstuffed chair. His sword, even cocked back, got in the way, so he unbuckled it and laid it beside him. Reginald waited for him to say more, but he didn't.

"Where is Karl?" Reginald asked.

"Bed. The train thing was a kind of assassination. Karl was a target."

Reginald nodded. He knew.

"We think that the Romanian Deacon is dead. It's hard to tell through the human bullshit. They'll probably blame this on terrorism, but they know. They know that vampires caused it, and they know that a team of vampires walked through the wreckage and methodically killed all of the survivors. They'll be livid. Pitchforks and torches livid. Because we never got a chance to talk, they won't know we were on board, and that the Romanian Council may have lost its Deacon. They'll only see the cost in human life, which was substantial."

Nikki's eyes were in the corners of their sockets. "Wait," she said. "How was the Romanian guy coming from Luxembourg City?"

Maurice's head fell. He put his face in his palms.

"That's right; you don't know," he said as if it had just occurred to him. "*Three* trains were derailed tonight. All at about the same time. All three of the trains were headed into Paris for the summit. And we think more. Maybe derailments, but maybe other things. It's all a fog."

"*Three* trains?" said Nikki.

"*Maybe* other things?" said Reginald.

"Remember 9-11? How long it took for the authorities to sort through it all and determine that there were only four planes involved, instead of like a dozen that were reported at one time or another?"

Reginald remembered. Maurice had probably slept through the September 11, 2001 attacks, but Reginald had still been human at the time and quite vividly remembered watching it all unfold live. And Maurice was right; new reports had come in the whole time about additional planes, about bombs, about men on the ground. There was even a term for it, Reginald remembered: *The fog of war.*

Which meant, little as Reginald wanted to admit it, that the opening shots of a war had now been fired.

"What else?" said Reginald.

Maurice rubbed his head. "I'm very tired."

SKYPE

Maurice went to bed. Nikki washed up and did the same, giving Reginald a peck on the cheek before retiring. Reginald took her hand and held it for a few extra seconds, then gave her a grim smile and wished her goodnight, never having quite made the adjustment to "good day" or something more literal.

Then he sat with a laptop on his legs and settled in with cup of blood and coffee, knowing that he'd be up all day.

Slowly, a very large and very troubling story began to emerge. What he'd at first taken as a random act of terrorism by an angry vampire fringe group began to look more and more like a widespread, organized attempt to consolidate and seize power. What had at first seemed like a strike against the human population in the spirit of "only human" now looked like something that had been masterminded and carefully coordinated. Maurice's mention of September 11 clanged in Reginald's mind. Reginald remembered how he'd felt back then, human and vulnerable, as he'd heard about the first plane striking the first tower. When they'd started saying that it might be terrorism, he'd been afraid. If terrorists could turn a plane into a weapon, what could be more terrifying than that? But soon after he'd gotten his answer: terror-ists enacting a well-thought-out plan to turn *many* planes into *many* weapons. He could almost have gotten his head past the act of one small group of crazies, but it was much harder to wrap his mind around a group that had planned, and planned, and planned. It hadn't been done in the heat of the moment. It had taken years of hatred and premeditation and... and *evil*. It had sent a chill up his spine. It had changed the way he saw the world around him. Innocence was gone in an instant.

This felt that way. And even though Reginald was far less vulnerable as a vampire, he could still be killed. His friends could still be killed. And those humans? How many had died overnight? Reginald didn't know the capacity of a TGV train off the top of his head and refused to look it up because he knew it would only depress him, especially since he'd have to multiply it by three to find the grand total. What else was a group that evil capable of? What would they do next? Since the Ring of Fire, the world had become a very different place. A warning shot had been fired across the bow of vampirekind, and many vampires had taken that shot very, very seriously. Some had done as he and Maurice had, looking for new ways for the species to evolve. Others believed what Maurice's brother seemed to believe — that the only way to save all of their skins was to wipe out as many humans as possible, and to do whatever was necessary to disrupt plans to restore peace. After all, what was a summit but a wrench in the plans of the radical faction? The killing and turning had to continue. You couldn't have softies like Karl Stromm and the late Romanian Deacon meeting with human leaders to talk about peace. Let the war rage. Vampires would come out on top, right?

A ringing noise came from the laptop and a notification appeared in the corner of the screen:

INCOMING CALL FROM
CLAIRE

Reginald scrabbled on the trackpad, suddenly sure that he was going to miss the call despite it being right in front of him. It was a video call. He responded with video and a new window opened showing an empty room. Or, more accurately, a ceiling.

"Claire?" he said.

Nothing.

"Hey, Claire. Are you there?"

Reginald was suddenly seized by a certainty: Claire hadn't called at all. Soon he'd see a vampire's face fill the screen, his lips wet with blood. The vampire would smile, happy to have gotten a hit while scrolling through Claire's Skype contacts to gloat. And then the vampire would pick up the laptop and angle it toward Claire's dismembered corpse, her room covered in blood, and...

"Hey," said a small voice.

"Claire?" Reginald's breath caught in his throat. It felt like he'd been saved from a firing line. He hadn't realized how worried he was, and how worried he'd been ever since that night that Victoria had almost been killed, when Claire had disappeared from his life.

"Yeah."

"I can only see your ceiling."

"I know. I..."

"Are you okay?" A new certainty was blooming in Reginald's mind: she'd been attacked and disfigured. She was breaking him in to the idea slowly. Next he'd see her, but she'd be wearing a pillow-case over her head with eyeholes cut through it so that he couldn't see the slash marks that had been made by teeth or fangs.

"What?" An irritated, exasperated noise. "No, seriously, what the hey, Reginald. I'm just... " She sighed. *"Fine."*

The screen tilted and he saw Claire's face. And it was indeed disfigured.

"I couldn't figure out how to turn off the video to call and I didn't want to... *ugh*." She touched the huge pimple that was directly in the middle of her forehead like a hindu dot. It was one of the huge ones that started deep and would hurt to touch.

Reginald almost chuckled, but held it in. This was all very fragile.

"Aren't you a little young for zits?" he said.

Claire shrugged. "I'm a little young for a lot of things, but…" She trailed off, giving a *What can you do?* shrug. Reginald sensed there was more behind it, but he didn't pry.

"It's good to hear from you," he said.

Claire shrugged again.

"I've been worried."

"I can take care of myself."

She always had, but she shouldn't have had to. It was unfair that just as she was getting her mother back, her mother was incapacitated by vampires. Claire would never admit it, but that was clearly the reason she'd spent three months being angry and refusing to talk to anyone with fangs, regardless of their intention: she'd finally let her guard down and had dared to hope… and just look at what had happened.

"I guess you can," said Reginald.

Claire said nothing, looking everywhere but at the screen or her webcam. It was as if she'd been forced to call and didn't want to. But nobody else was in the room, and even at eleven, Claire had never seemed big on doing what anyone told her to.

"How's your mom?"

"Bad," Claire spat.

"Bad?"

Claire sighed as if admitting something she didn't want to admit. "I guess she's maybe a little better. But still not good. She's tired all the time like she's anemic."

"Anemic?"

"I know what anemic means," she snapped. "I'm not an idiot."

Reginald raised his hands to the screen. "I know you know what it means. I just meant, does it seem like she's always light-headed, despite the fact that the doctors keep saying she's received enough blood and that her counts are okay?"

"Lightheaded. Stupid. She can barely remember my name. She can't cook because she'll burn the house down. I have to make her sandwiches and then remind her to eat them. All we do is watch soap operas. I haven't been going to school. Nobody seems to care."

Reginald nodded. He'd figured that much already. When the world started to slide into shit, things like keeping track of school attendance started to matter less and less.

"It's something in our saliva," said Reginald. "Nobody's bothered to figure out exactly what it is or give it a proper name, but it's referred to casually as 'the agent.' It works like spider venom and does something short of temporarily paralyzing the victim. And it lasts in the blood for a long time, especially in bad attacks by multiple vampires. But it *does* go away. She *will* get better, and return to her own self."

The video's resolution was quite clear — clear enough that Reginald could see Claire's lips purse in frustration and anger. A tear ran down the side of her nose, unheeded.

"I'm sorry," said Reginald. "On behalf of all of us."

"Was it because I knew you? Did they attack her because I was Deacon Maurice's and Deputy Reginald's little pet?"

Reginald didn't want to seem too defensive and protest too much, so he said, carefully, "I don't know. But I don't think so. This kind of thing is happening everywhere. The whole Vampire Nation is going through a..."

"I dreamed you were in a train crash," she said. "All three of you."

Reginald stopped mid-sentence, his mouth hanging open. He wondered if Claire had seen the news through her regimen of soap operas. The story of the trio of high-speed rail derailments headed into Paris was all over the news. In America it wouldn't have the panicked, terrorism-tinged fever pitch it had in Europe, but there was no question they'd be reporting it. But nobody knew that they were on one of those trains. Nobody human or still alive, anyway.

"It was at night," Claire continued. "You were on a train going like hundreds of miles an hour, and you hit something and all of the cars came off the track. Everyone was killed. You were hurt. I remember very distinctly dreaming that you had to chew off your own arm. Then you had to hide, because... because of *something*. Something was trying to get you. And that's all I remember."

She turned to the camera. Reginald stared at his screen, into her eyes. Because of the positions of the cameras, each would feel like they were staring into eyes that were looking just off the screen. Without being face-to-face, this was as close as they'd get to a sincere heart-to-heart.

"That actually happened," said Reginald. "Exactly like that."

"I know."

"You saw the news?"

Claire gave a sad little purse-lipped smile and tapped her head: *I just know.*

Reginald had been waiting for something like this, wondering how the gifts that he knew were within her would manifest. She had a unique pedigree, being only the second person fathered by an incubus and born of a human woman. The other, according to legend, had been King Arthur's sorcerer Merlin. Reginald had spent a lot of time thinking about that and had decided that despite all of the fantasy that had surrounded Arthurian legend over the years, Merlin had almost surely been real. He probably hadn't carried a Gandalf staff and blasted lightning from his palms, but he'd probably had real powers that had become exaggerated over the years, walking through the centuries and growing like a game of Telephone.

"It's starting," he said. "What we talked about."

"That and the zits." She pointed at the giant red spot on her forehead.

It made sense. Claire was probably still a few years shy of

adolescence (how shy of it he wouldn't know without asking questions that he shouldn't and wouldn't ask) but it seemed logical that if whatever power was within her had laid dormant all these years, that it might be the changes during adolescence that would trigger them. He thought of the crack she'd made the last time they'd been together (the last time they'd spoken, in fact) about how maybe Reginald's own mystery — the bolt of something fired into his head by the angel Balestro which still hadn't manifested — would show up when *he* reached puberty.

"How long has it been going on?"

"A few weeks. It's... it scares me."

So that was why she'd called. Was her addled human mother going to understand her daughter's blossoming magic? Claire didn't have anyone else to talk to. Too many changes. She was just a little girl, and she was so small for her age. Despite her ferocity, Reginald had always wanted to protect her — always from a distance, because she'd never accept pity.

"What else can you do?" he asked. "Telepathy? Moving things with your mind? Making *The Simpsons* funny again?"

"Mostly dreams," she answered. "But I know when I'm having them that they're real. It's like... I don't know. They're mostly stupid, useless things. The other night I woke up in the middle of the night and turned down the volume on my alarm clock because I'd realized it was turned up full-tilt and it was going to scare me to death when it went off. But then there's also this."

Claire stuck out her tongue.

Reginald leaned toward the screen, missing the point. "Wait," he said. "I didn't see anything. Stick your tongue out again."

"No... Reginald..." she said, "I *didn't* stick out my tongue. That's the point."

Reginald felt his forehead wrinkle. "What?"

"Just now. You saw me stick out my tongue, right? But I *didn't* stick out my tongue. Here... watch this."

She reached forward on the desk and came back with a

cellular phone in her hand. She pressed a few buttons, then held it at arm's length in front of her, with the lens pointed back at her face.

"Okay, ready? Now watch my face." And again, on Reginald's screen, she stuck out her tongue.

"So far, so good," said Reginald.

Claire turned the phone to face her and pressed more buttons. Then she turned the camera so that its screen was facing and close to the webcam. The video was already playing. On the small screen of the phone, Claire said, "Okay, ready? Now watch my face." But this time, on the phone's video, she closed her eyes for a moment and seemed to concentrate. Offscreen, Reginald heard himself say, "So far, so good." The video blurred with motion and then ended.

Reginald blinked. "That's astonishing," he said. "I wouldn't have believed it if you hadn't just shown me the side-by-side. And I'm still not convinced you didn't stage an elaborate joke just to fu... to *mess* with me. How did you do that?"

"It just happens. I discovered it when I was making a YouTube video. Every time I did a take, I laughed because I was nervous. Then I finally did one where I didn't laugh, but when I looked at the video, I saw myself laughing. I figured I had the wrong video, but then I did it three more times. It's like what I think about ends up... I don't know... pushing things around on the computer. I can open and close windows too. Sometimes I can type."

Reginald shook his head. After all he'd seen in the past year, he was beyond being outright shocked by something so amazing, but he couldn't help being impressed. He'd heard about telekinetics who could move objects with their mind, but he'd never before heard of anyone who could create pictures — such vivid, real pictures — from their mind.

What Reginald didn't tell Claire — because it was dangerous and because she might not be old enough to handle it — was that if she could harvest thoughts from a distance and if she could manipulate complex signals in a computer, she might be able to influence the thoughts of others. She might be able to push people to do things. Thoughts were just energy and signals, after all. If she could influence thoughts, it would be like glamouring, but potentially much stronger. It wasn't something that an eleven-year-old girl should experiment with.

"So what do I do, Reginald?"

He shook his head again. "I don't know."

"You haven't heard about any abilities like this? Not amongst vampires, incubuses, werewolves..."

"Werewolves aren't real. What do you think this is, some stupid horror story?"

Claire wadded up a piece of paper and threw it at the webcam. Reginald took it as a good sign. It seemed playful. Maybe she'd gotten her anger out and was ready to stop holding a grudge. Reginald would like that. He'd like having his ward back. And hell... he'd like to have that ability on *his* side, since it seemed more and more likely that there *would* be sides in the coming months and years, for better or for worse.

"I've never heard of anything like those abilities, Claire. They make you very unique, and all you can do is wait. Do I have to remind you to use your powers for good instead of evil?"

"I'm joining the Justice Force."

"That's good. Its headquarters are here, in Luxembourg. So what we'll do is..."

She was shaking her head.

Reginald let her finish, waited a moment, and then spoke. "Did you actually shake your head, or are you demonstrating again?"

"I can't go there. My mom, Reginald."

Reginald shrugged. "*My* mom is here. You'd bring her with you."

"There's also our house. Our stuff. Our lives."

"Exactly," said Reginald. "Your *lives*. What's it like out on your streets?"

Claire sighed and gave a small, resolute shrug. It was a very adult gesture.

"So that's it. You've decided already?" he asked.

"We can't leave. You... you don't know, Reginald. We have family and friends here. And you can't know what it's like to only have this one little thing that you fought for. We've never had much. This is the life we have. It's... it's *all* we have."

"But as it gets worse out there..."

"We'll be okay. I'll call you every day."

"But I can't be there in time if something happens," he said.

Claire actually laughed. "You're not exactly a great bodyguard anyway, Reginald. And I say that in the best, most affectionate way possible."

Reginald felt a spark of irritation and suppressed an urge to remind Claire that the only reason her mother was alive was because he'd intervened. The rednecks couldn't have saved her in time. Even fat old Reginald had his uses.

Instead, he said, "I guess."

"I'll call every day," she repeated.

Reginald took a deep, resigned sigh. He could work on her. He could convince her over time. Rome wasn't built in a day, no matter what those damn Romans said.

"Fine," he said. "But do it closer to nighttime. I need my beauty sleep."

Claire touched her giant red zit, remarked that she needed it too, and laughed.

CIVILIZED

The day after the TGV attacks, Nicholas Timken contacted William Erickson, a human magistrate of little notice in the formal human political world but of considerable power in the area of human/vampire relations, to extend an olive branch in the spirit of interspecies cooperation. The story trended at the top of all of the vampire social networks and news outlets. It was heralded not only as admirable, but also as extremely gutsy.

Following the disaster, a heavy curtain of ice had fallen between the vampire and human worlds. It had the feel of cutting off, of forever drawing a line between the two camps — who, it was assumed, would both begin preparing for war. The humans knew that vampires had begun widespread, highly-coordinated attacks and required immediate retaliation. The vampires knew that humans would blame all vampires for the acts of a few, and that the best defense against an inevitable human retaliation would be a good offense.

Vampires authorities rallied other vampires in preparation for unbridled massacre. Human authorities readied the secret, highly-trained Anti-Vampire Taskforce shock troops — the modern descendants of villagers with pitchforks and torches.

Nobody spoke. The world held its breath, and waited.

But in that icy atmosphere, as calm as anything, Timken had phoned Erickson. Insiders on both sides reported being shocked by the stupendously naive nature of the call. It was as if Timken didn't realize that everyone in Erickson's office wanted to stake every vampire in existence, including Timken himself. It was as if Timken didn't realize that he was being a total and complete asshole in calling. And Erickson, shocked by the move, had found himself listening to and then accepting Timken's offer to send half of his now-800-strong Sedition Army troops to seek out those responsible for the "acts of wanton terrorism." Troops headed out. Talk began anew. And slowly, tentatively, the world began to exhale.

Back on the home front, at Vampire Nation HQ, Councilman Brian Nickerson had returned to the Council. This had not happened lightly. Timken had reached out to all of the departed Council members via Fangbook, and then Brian, unsure what to think, had reached out to Maurice via Fangbook. After a week with no response, he then reached out to Nikki via Fangbook, and Nikki reported that Maurice never, ever checked his Fangbook inbox. Brian replied to Nikki: *LOL I knew that WTF.* Then he told Nikki about Timken's message and asked what they knew about the new Council, the temporary Deacon, and whether or not he'd be safe to return. Nikki replied, for all three of them, that they didn't know. Brian said that he had nothing better to do. He told them that he would flip a coin. Apparently he did flip that coin and it came up heads, because a few days later Nikki had a new Fangbook message from Brian, reporting that he'd returned to Columbus.

On his first day back at Council, Brian Skyped the Chateau with his report.

"He's rebuilt the infrastructure under the Asbury — which, by the way, his group apparently bought. It's nice down here," he said. On video, he looked around the room, pointing changes out to the webcam. "He changed the layout. Because it won't move every ten fucking days anymore, he's making it much nicer and more permanent. There's a game room now. And by the way, news flash: vampires aren't meant to play ping-pong. The ball can't move fast enough for those of us who've played, and when we try to make it move faster, we keep destroying the ball."

"Vampires play ping-pong?" said Reginald, who hadn't been paying much attention.

"Apparently Timken lived with humans for a while and learned it from them. But he was always playing against humans and slowed himself down, so this problem never showed up."

"Timken lived with humans?" said Nikki. "And played ping-pong with them?"

"He's a do-gooder," said Karl, who'd walked up behind them, with a bit more venom than seemed necessary. Brian had never met Karl before. Karl hovered for a while and then left without introducing himself. When Karl turned to go, Brian said, "See ya, Dracula."

"Oh, and check *this* out," said Brian, reaching forward and rotating the camera to show the far side of the room. Along one wall was a full-size vintage Pac-Man video game, a pinball machine, and two large cabinets with glass fronts. Reginald reached forward and touched the screen.

"Are those vending machines?"

"Yup. Pouches of the best blood. And Bloodsicles in the freezer one. There's even some human food, but nobody has touched it. Like..."

"I see... *Ho-Hos,*" said Reginald. His fangs came out. He covered his mouth self-consciously as if he'd just popped a boner in class.

The camera rotated back and showed Brian's face. Reginald felt sad, as if he'd lost something.

"You should come back," said Brian. "I've visited with Charles.

He's in one of the old holding cells, along with your boy Walker. There's no threat to you here anymore."

Reginald thought of the last time they'd been at the Council. The entire Guard corps had turned rogue and were calling themselves Kill Squads. Every vampire in the building had come at them with their fangs bared, then had tried to chase them into the sun and rip them apart. Maurice had been threatened every day as Deacon. And now, behind Brian, a few vampires were milling about as if everything were totally normal and no-harm-done, but Reginald forced himself to remember that the "normal" he saw was merely a thin veneer covering the murderous chaos that had reigned with the same group not two weeks ago. Civilization, thought Reginald, could be much like a Band-Aid.

"I think we'll hang out here for a little longer," said Maurice, giving Reginald a look that said he knew exactly what Reginald had been thinking.

Brian reported more good news. He said that the demeanor in the Council and in the streets had taken a 180-degree turn. It seemed, he said, as if the population just needed someone in charge to tell them that everything was going to be all right. It was a lie, of course — war was still heavy on many human and vampire lips, and the Ring of Fire incident was still far from understood or forgotten — but as Maurice himself had pointed out the last time he'd been at Council, sometimes people preferred a beautiful lie to the horrible truth. Brian added with an optimistic smile that the same vampires who had been ripping open the throats of random humans and painting with their blood a few weeks ago were now back to wearing their fashionable dark suits, combing their hair, and spending all their time preening and making sexual innuendo while acting vastly superior.

"All it took to change everything entirely was a change in perception," said Brian.

"Yes, that's all it took," Reginald agreed. But while Brian meant it as a positive thing, the fickle nature of the population's temperament was exactly what scared the bejesus out of Reginald. A vampire could be a killer one moment and totally civilized the next. And that was great, until you remembered that the switch could flip in both directions. If Reginald could throw a vampire, which he very much couldn't, he would have uttered the aphorism about not trusting any among the Council any further than he could throw them.

"You don't trust them any further than *I* can throw them," said Nikki helpfully.

"You could throw them a half mile," said Reginald. "I don't trust them a half mile."

Nikki shook her head. "That doesn't make any sense."

"*Exactly*," said Reginald with a suspicious look.

With Timken's men's help, the human authorities soon located fourteen vampires believed to behind the TGV attacks. AVT troops stormed a dark bar that was reportedly the headquarters of their group of dissonants and found all fourteen vampire men and women together. The vampires attempted to attack the human soldiers, but they were unable to harm them through the specially designed armor that all of the AVT wore. Still, the vampires were too fast to catch, and a standoff ensued. Eventually the Sedition Army troops stationed outside moved in and used their Boom Stick weapons. None of the AVT or SA troops were injured. There were no dissonant survivors. Files were found on-site that speculated about weak spots in the high-speed rail system from an engineering standpoint. Calendars with key dates marked. Maps. Plots and plans.

The public cheered.

And back in the US, Timken kept his word about the upcoming free elections. A date was set; technology was put in place; the vampires of the Nation were informed and educated on the process. All voting was to occur through Fangbook — a system that impartial vampires declared to be imperturbable. Fangbook wasn't like human Facebook. No individual could have two accounts, and profiles were indexed to a user's blood. It was secure. It was fair.

"Do you buy it?" Nikki asked Reginald once while they were watching election coverage on Vampire YouTube.

Reginald, his eyes on the screen and a slice of pizza in his hand, nodded slowly. "Believe it," he said. "Fangbook is arguably the most powerful force in the vampire world. You know how it's indexed by blood and how everyone has an account whether they use it or not?" He tapped the screen. "If you worry about Big Brother, worry about this. Maurice doesn't know everyone he's related to by blood. But Fangbook does."

But despite the Big Brother implications, Reginald had nothing further to say about Fangbook and its know-it-all status. His bigger concerns were Charles, who seemed to be both contained and being granted his reluctant rights, and Timken, who did indeed seem to be playing fair.

"Yes, there is good news and bad news here," said Reginald. "The person who wins this election will be the vampire who most of the voters want to win."

"Is that the good news or the bad news?" said Nikki.

Reginald took another bite of his pizza and chewed, watching Fangbook's master feed scroll past. "Both."

Reginald's chief concern was the fact that he didn't trust most vampires (not farther than he could throw them, anyway) and was certain that whoever they chose would be, in Reginald's words, "An insufferable asshole."

Nikki, always the optimist, disagreed. She opened a Fangbook election page and tapped it just as Reginald had done earlier. "Look at this list of candidates," she said. "It's miles long. Anyone can get on the ballot."

"This is supposed to make me feel better?" said Reginald.

"Brian is on here. Maurice is on here. Hell, someone even nominated you. The nomination says, 'He has a hot ass.' "

"You did that."

"You don't know that, hot ass."

"There are no good choices," said Reginald, nonplussed. "All we can hope for is a *less shitty* leader."

"Well, isn't that what humans do?"

Reginald laughed at that.

But despite the miles-long nomination list, sentiment two weeks prior to the formal Fangbook election was clearly divided across three candidates. As things stood, forty-seven percent were predicted to vote for Timken. A very dark and disturbing thirty-one percent backed the master of chaos, Charles Barkley. Five percent wanted Maurice to take the reins back, which Maurice found flattering but laughable and "not gonna happen." The rest were undecided.

"Those," said Reginald, pointing at the "undecided" wedge on a pre-election pie chart, "are the only vampires with their heads screwed on straight."

Maurice punched him. "Don't be a dick. Timken is going to win, and that's fine. That's the best we could do under the circumstances."

But Reginald didn't know. He didn't trust authority. Not anymore. And maybe never again.

HOT AIR

On the biggest preliminary night leading up to the vampire election — the night the leading candidates would make their speeches — Karl had a formal banquet prepared at the Chateau. A large, ancient-looking and beautiful wooden table was placed in the cathedral room with twenty-four wooden chairs around it. Dozens of other chairs were placed around smaller tables. The largest, most comfortable chairs were placed in groups in the corners, creating cozy enclaves.

The banquet fare consisted of dozens of sushi girls and guys. The one departure from normal sushi served off of a person was that instead of lying naked on the tables covered in sushi, these appetizers laid on the tables without any sushi covering them, completely naked. And because there wasn't enough room on the table for dozens of naked donors unless they were stacked tall like poker chips (an arrangement that Karl considered aesthetically displeasing), most of them roamed the room like nude waiters, carrying trays of garnishes (wine, strawberries, and flavored skin lotions, all of which went well with blood and were recently in vogue at high-end vampire bloodspots) and bending their necks for whoever wanted a taste. The gathering was an odd mishmash of nude humans and posh, formal vampires. It was as if a party planner had decided to split-test two very different dress codes at once.

Reginald's finery consisted of a twenty year-old Izod golf shirt that had made its way into his luggage by mistake. It was too small, but he'd squeezed himself into it like sausage into a casing. Nikki had done much better. She hadn't packed any dress clothes from home either, but she'd visited a chic boutique on a weekend trip to Paris and had spent a used Volkswagen's worth of Euros on a dress that made her look a hot cartoon character. It was jet black, with wonderful boost and exposure at her cleavage, widest at the hips and pixie-thin toward her feet so that she had to shuffle when she walked. She looked fantastic when she was standing still. The effect was magnified if she held something seductively out at her side with her palm up, and she'd expressed regret while dressing that she didn't buy a cigarette holder to use as a prop. Reginald gave her one of the shish kebabs that were out for the Chateau's human guests and for a while she'd held that, but she abandoned it when several of the human guests (mostly Reginald's mother) walked over to Nikki, thanked her, and took an item off of the end of the shish kebab to eat. So Nikki had traded the shish kebab in for a simpler prop — a full-bodied wine-glass filled with some of Karl's vintage O positive. She didn't trust herself to walk around with the glass and made Reginald hold it when she wanted to mingle. This was wise. She fell repeatedly.

Karl, true to Karl form, wore a fantastic robe that looked both a thousand years old and priceless. It was Asian, with a high collar that stood up very high around his neck. Maurice commented that it looked like he was wearing a halo so that he wouldn't chew at his stitches when he came home from the veterinarian's office. Karl scoffed and said something insulting about Maurice having lived in America for too long.

A very large screen had been hung on the side wall of the room. On the screen was the Vampire News Network feed, currently showing muted pre-election coverage. From time to time, the screen would flash the faces of the candidates: Timken, Charles, and Maurice. Maurice thought this was absurd. His base of support was ridiculously small, and he wouldn't be giving a speech both because he was in Europe and because he didn't want to be on the ballot. But the network seemed to enjoy the idea of a three-party race despite the obviousness of the outcome, so it cycled through the backstories of all of them. The screen showed Timken shaking hands with well-known vampire businessmen, then the famous footage of Timken standing on a chair during the coup. It showed footage of Charles's free-for-all Council days and his one dramatic speech slamming "the old regime." The last piece of video in the rotation was a flattering clip of Maurice giving a speech at Council. Maurice looked good, which was unusual. Normally he looked ridiculous in the Deacon's box, as if someone's teenager had sneaked into it to shout stupid things at the assembly — things like "Baba Booey."

Reginald milled the party, feeling awkward. He'd never been good at things like this. Even with a beautiful woman on his arm it was difficult. And to make matters worse, said beautiful woman kept tripping over her dress and falling down, which drew every-one's attention. Not that anyone cared. Halfway through the gathering, Nikki spilled a giant punchbowl filled with a blood-and-fruit concoction, and when she did, several of the intoxicated partygoers fell to the floor and started licking at it, their move-ments filling with more and more sexual innuendo until they started biting each other and having sex on the floor. Those who were interested watched and clapped and reached down to touch. The rest ignored them and continued to mill as if nothing out of the ordinary was happening.

Eventually Karl called for order. The room slowly quieted and all eyes looked toward the tall man in the extravagant robe. The vampires writhing in the blood and fruit on the floor didn't stop, but did courteously decrease the volume of their sex and biting.

Karl raised his hands. It looked like he might make a grand proclamation, but instead he said, "Let us watch the Americans make the bullshit" and gave a nod to someone across the room. The news feed was unmuted. A reporter onscreen (Reginald assumed she was a vampire, but there was no way to tell) finished a prepared bit about free elections for the first time ever, then took a moment to mention the world's appreciation of Timken for his help in investigating the TGV attacks. She didn't outright say that Timken had saved the American Vampire Nation (and, she implied, the entire vampire world) from Charles Barkley's gaping asshole, but it wasn't hard to read between the lines.

The reporter then concluded by saying that two of the candidates would be speaking shortly but that the third to meet the five percent prediction minimum, Deacon Maurice Toussant, was not in attendance and would not be speaking tonight.

"I'd rather eat the food Reginald eats," said Maurice. He was standing behind Reginald, squeezed into what looked like a cheap prom tux from a Tuxedo Junction in a mall. He even had a pocket square. His hair looked oily, but for a change, his face didn't.

"Me too," said Reginald.

While the group in the Chateau watched, Charles Barkley took the stage. He looked like someone who'd gotten cleaned up but couldn't hide how gross he was at the core. Once upon a time, Charles had been incredibly handsome, as were all vampires in the decades preceding Reginald. But now, something had changed. Even Reginald, with his mind regaining its razor's edge, couldn't tell what. Charles was, of course, incapable of actual *physical* change. He couldn't have lost or gained weight; he couldn't have had any plastic surgery. But the change also didn't seem to be the presence of or absence of makeup. It didn't seem to be his hair; it didn't seem to be his clothes; it didn't seem to be the lighting in the room. Against all logic, Reginald finally decided that what he was seeing on Charles was the stink of evil. The whole world knew what a son of a bitch he was, how lazy and power-hungry he was, and where the Nation would go under his leadership. Now that Timken had restored order, the Nation's time spent under Charles stood out like a bloody and pulverized thumb.

Charles's speech was about desperate times calling for desperate measures. He talked a lot about the need to be afraid during these "days of trial." This made both Karl and Maurice roll their eyes and hurl insults at the screen. Nikki and Reginald, by contrast, simply watched, wondering between them if it was working, if any of the audience was being scared over to Charles's side. And the answer was: almost certainly.

But when Timken took the stage, Reginald's concerns about Charles's ability to control the Nation with fear vanished. Timken's speech was *all about* fear, but instead of telling the viewers that they should be afraid, he told them how frightened he himself had been when he'd seen that ominous Ring of Fire form in front of his eyes. The mental picture he painted was brilliantly moving. Reginald found himself returning to that night on the hilltop, feeling his own fear. He'd experienced that terror. He'd experienced that helplessness. But at least Reginald had been there with Balestro as he'd created the Ring, and had felt some modicum of control. At least Reginald, at the time, had had a plan. The vampires of the world hadn't had any of that. They'd simply stared onrushing death in its unblinking eye and had held their breath, waiting to die.

The vampires in the Chateau, listening, had gone still. All eyes were on the screen — or, perhaps more accurately, all eyes were looking back to the day that they'd seen that Ring. The day they'd realized that it could all be over in a second, and that there was nothing they could do about it.

Then, Timken talked about the anarchy that had ruled the Nation for the past few months. He talked about his opponent, taking the high road and being careful not to malign Charles so as to allow viewers to malign him in their own minds. He explained that chaos and mayhem were one way they could react to a threat, but that it was the easy way out... and as usual, the *easy* way wasn't the *right* way.

"Are we insects?" he said, his voice high and strong, power and pride radiating from him as it had the day he'd stood on that chair during his coup, holding an ordinary human firearm high as a symbol. "Or are we predators? Will we cower, or will we rise up? The future is coming. The judgment of our creators is coming. We will face trials and tribulations and harsh decisions. The next years may not be easy. They may be very, very difficult. They may test our cores as beings. But will we face those hard times as frightened animals with our backs curled around our middles, our faces hidden, our spines exposed for the taking? Or will we stand tall and face them as one, unified, our shoulders back and our fangs out?" His fangs descended. His eyes seemed to redden. His voice rose, tremulous and hectoring as he finished with a fist held high, shouting with defiant pride: "ARE WE COWARDS? *OR ARE WE VAMPIRES?*"

The entire council chamber erupted into cheers. Even Reginald's mother raised a fist. Reginald liked to think that she was doing it in solidarity for her son, but he suspected that right now, for this one and only moment in time, she was probably wishing to be turned so that she could develop vampire-enhanced powers of passive aggressiveness.

"Check this out," said Nikki, holding out an arm. "I got goosebumps. Literal *goosebumps*. I never got them as a human and figured I'd missed my chance."

Onscreen, Timken was raising both hands, pumping both fists in the air with a stern, unamused expression on his face. He looked singlemindedly determined, unfazed by the applause that had erupted. Then the shot switched to the reporter again, whose face had flushed and who did a poor job of pretending to be impartial. She commented on how "lively" tonight's speeches were. She said that it was shaping up to be "quite a race."

"Don't judge me," Maurice was saying to Karl, "but I kind of feel like punching through a wall."

"Refrain," said Karl, his face still stoic and unimpressed, "or you'll collapse the cave and kill us all."

When Karl was gone, Maurice smiled to Nikki and Reginald. "He just doesn't want me to mess up his pretty tapestries. We wouldn't die if this room collapsed."

Reginald, thinking of being trapped in the TGV wreckage, said nothing.

"I think he'll be good for us," said Maurice. "You know, better than me. Better than Charles. Better than Logan."

"Better than nothing," said Reginald.

"Yeah, right."

"But the one thing Charles had going for him tonight," said Reginald, "is that he described what he wanted to do about the Ring of Fire issue."

"Yeah," said Maurice. "Kill and turn. Probably lead us into outright war with humans. That plan sounds great."

"Oh, yeah, it's a terrible plan," said Reginald.

Maurice stopped grinning and looked at Reginald. Reginald's eyes were still on the screen. A male voice was explaining that just as in the American human system, the new Deaconship structure called for a true Vice Deacon to share responsibility for governing and as a check on power, and added that the candidates would be announcing their Vice picks shortly.

"But?" said Maurice.

"But Timken didn't give any specifics about his plan at all," Nikki answered for Reginald.

"I guess he was going more for hearts and minds," said Maurice.

Reginald, saying nothing and still watching the screen, nodded slowly.

Maurice started to reply, but then he stopped. His mouth hung open. He stared with eyes like saucers. Charles was back on the screen. He'd just announced his running mate — the vampire who would become his Vice Deacon if he were to win.

It was Todd Walker.

"No," said Maurice.

They had only seen about an hour of Walker as a vampire. It had happened back when Walker had first been turned, back at their old office building after a group of vampires had killed off most of Reginald, Maurice, and Nikki's co-workers. But the assailants hadn't done all of the killing. A good number of the dead had been murdered by Walker himself. And on that first night, he'd shown them how dangerous he would be as a vampire — and how potentially deadly he'd be as he grew older and stronger.

Reginald, who'd seen this coming, kept nodding.

"We should have killed him," said Maurice, eyeing Nikki. Maurice had *wanted* to kill him. He'd actually had his hands on the sides of Walker's head, ready to twist it off, when Nikki had stopped him.

Nikki didn't fire back at Maurice. They'd had this debate many times before.

"Charles isn't going to win," she said.

"So?" Maurice blurted.

"So Walker won't have any more power than he already has."

"It doesn't matter. You know how politics are. He can parlay this. They're going to keep holding elections, you know. True, it won't be Charles and Walker this time. But what if, a few years down the road, it *is* Walker? What then? What if it takes him a hundred years to find his power? He wants it. You know he does; you worked beside him for years. And now he has the profile from being Charles's man, and he has that seductive, persuasive personality, and he's got..."

Maurice stopped when Reginald put a hand on his shoulder. Reginald's other hand was on Nikki's shoulder. Nikki and Maurice, engaged in fierce debate, stopped looking at each other and instead looked at Reginald. Now *Reginald's* mouth was hanging open. Now *Reginald's* eyes were saucers staring at the giant screen.

"What is it?" said Nikki.

"Look," said Reginald.

All three of them looked up. Onscreen, Nicholas Timken had just introduced his own running mate to the camera.

It was Maurice's brother, Claude.

ANNIHILIST SONS OF BITCHES

Nikki's fangs sank into Reginald's neck, bringing sharp pain. She wrapped her legs around him and pushed off of one of the walls, propelling them both across the room and into the opposite wall, shattering a ceramic lamp and ripping its shade. Reginald's back struck rock. His head rang with impact. With the lamp broken and only a small endtable light still on, the room fell into hideous rocking shadows.

"Ow, hell!" Reginald blurted.

"Shut up," she spat, taking her teeth from his neck for long enough to berate him. "Shut up and give it to me."

Nikki's strong vampire legs squeezed him so hard he thought she might cut him in half. Her long nails punctured the skin on his back. He could feel lines of blood running down his ample ass. He was quite sure he could feel skin peeling away under her fingernails, curling up at the end of a long scratch like wood shaved off by a wood planer. It was technically sex that they were having, but it felt more like an mixed martial arts fight — or perhaps as if Nikki had never experienced either sex or torture and had gotten them confused.

"Sure," said Reginald. "Consider it given to you."

Nikki unwrapped one leg and used it to trip Reginald while she continued to bite him. They fell to the floor, hard, and broke the side off of an endtable. Reginald felt the wind knocked out of himself and fought for breath. Nikki took his pain for arousal and bit him harder. The impact of her head on the stone floor had apparently split her scalp, and a small pool of blood had formed before she'd healed. Reginald knew she could feel pain just fine, but she seemed over the past months to have decided that for a vampire, pain was truly temporary. There was really no decent reason to avoid something that would only hurt for a moment.

Nikki seemed unsatisfied.

"If you don't fuck me harder, I'm going to rip off your goddamn head!" she screamed.

"Oh, indeed," said Reginald. Then he tried, but really he was just smothering her.

Nikki groaned in frustration, kicked her legs behind her, and pushed hard, and threw them into the ceiling. Reginald had the sensation of breaking vertebrae as his back struck the stone, and then they ricocheted and landed on the bed, all four legs of which immediately exploded into shards. The entire bed frame struck the floor and the mattress knocked askew, Nikki rolling onto the top, Reginald beneath her and feeling like he should perhaps call an abuse hotline.

He hung in there, aware that he was at least somewhat aroused in the way a person could be aware that he was a little cold, and waited for it to end.

There was more biting and clawing, and then Nikki gave an award-worthy series of orgasmic screams, climbed off of Reginald, and put her fist through the wall. Then she briskly pulled her pants and shirt back on and opened the door. Maurice was standing outside with his hair blown back, looking like a man who's just had a bomb go off in his face.

"I feel better now," said Nikki, turning and marching back into the room.

Reginald had pulled his pants back on, sexually unsatisfied but satisfied plenty to simply be free. He sat up on the annihilated bed. Maurice remained in the doorway.

"I said, I'm fine," said Nikki, sitting in a chair.

Maurice looked over at Reginald. "You okay, man?"

Reginald thought about the question, then nodded slowly. "I'll be all right."

Still looking unsure, Maurice walked into the room and took the last remaining chair. The three of them formed a rough triangle. Maurice looked up at a large bloodstain on the ceiling that was roughly the size and shape of Reginald's torso and head.

"So he's behind the TGV derailments," said Nikki, businesslike, her fury at discovering Timken's subterfuge seemingly assuaged. "That's for sure."

Reginald thought, then nodded again. "Not for sure. But ninety-nine percent. If I had to guess, it was a high-pass series of assassinations disguised as terrorism. I'd thought about that from the beginning. Seven of the twelve people due at the aborted Paris summit were on those three trains — four humans and three vampires. Two of the vampires escaped — Karl and Solov."

"Solov is dead," said Maurice. "He was staked by a member of his own staff, supposedly. Just this morning."

Reginald took a slow breath.

"Just to disrupt the summit?" said Nikki. "But why? It's asking for war."

"*Maybe* to disrupt the summit. Or maybe to consolidate power. 'Cut of the head of the beast' and all of that. If Solov is gone, I'd say that almost all of Asia and is without a leader. Africa too. But let's be honest. America is the big dog in the vampire world, despite having the youngest population. As goes America, so goes the world."

"And America is going Timken," said Nikki.

Maurice shook his head. "In a sick way, I was hoping that Claude was the head of this TGV thing. Just because it made sense. He led crews marching through the wreckage, killing survivors. He's always been a sick, Annihilist son of a bitch."

"Annihilist?"

"Yes. The Annihilist Faction is a very old group with very old roots. It's changed a little over the years — gotten more sophisticated toys and better organization, for instance — but its mission has never changed. They want to eliminate humanity as the dominant presence on this planet. They want to go back to the days when vampires caught humans, restrained them, and farmed them for blood. Then they want to go further, and eliminate the rest. But it's always been a twisted pipe dream for them, like the psychos who talk about killing the president and and taking over the government. There simply aren't enough of them to make it remotely realistic, but they've always been a very troublesome little minority, and they've perpetrated huge mass murders, always threatening to expose us to the greater human population and angering those who know we exist. But the Annihilsts don't care. They *want* war, because they're sure they can win. They're insulted that humanity dominates this planet. They think it's a great moral wrong. They want to walk in the open and to rule cities as vampires in the way that the humans do now."

"I don't know about any mass killings by vampires," said Nikki.

"Of course you do. Jonestown. Heaven's Gate. The Branch Davidians."

"Those were cults."

Maurice gave her a shrug. "The ability to influence media can be a powerful thing."

Reginald stood and began to pace the room. "I don't need to say that this isn't good, do I?"

"Go ahead," said Maurice.

"This isn't good," said Reginald.

"Now I feel complete," said Maurice.

Reginald raised one hand and began to count on his fingers.

"First, we have the assassination of vampire leaders. Second, we have the public extermination of... what?... hundreds or thousands of humans. And third, we have the derailment — no pun intended — of the summit that was supposed to prevent what seemed like an all-out human-vampire war."

"But Timken's restored some of those relations by reaching out to William Erickson," said Nikki.

"To help investigate his own crime, deflect blame, and position hundreds of trained vampire soldiers in the heart of the human Anti-Vampire Taskforce," said Maurice.

"And fourth," Reginald continued, raising another finger, "we have the support of someone who wants to spur war, clear the planet of humans, and farm those that remain for blood."

"'Support' is the wrong way to put it," said Maurice. "Claude is nobody's lackey. He and Timken are equal partners if they're anything. You think *I* have money? Wooden bullets were Claude's invention. He had the idea way back when we were first turned. Most new vampires, as you know, go through an identity crisis. Claude did not. He became one hundred percent vampire the minute he was turned and decided that he wanted to kill the people on the farms adjacent to ours and take their land because they were 'below our kind.' Turned out that the family to one side were vampires, and that it was their father who had created us. When I found that out, I wanted to get to know them. I wanted to meet my maker, quite literally. But Claude still wanted the land. He wanted to kill them, but the best weapons we had at the time were crossbows. Claude recalled that story years later, around the time I finally parted ways with him for good, when firearms were invented. He said that if only we'd had wooden bullets that would fit in these new weapons, we could have killed our vampire father. I'd forgotten all about that, but it was as if Claude been holding a grudge for over a thousand years. Anyway, centuries later, he finally got tired of dreaming and made those wooden bullets. And today, with that income stream plus some wise investments, he's fantastically wealthy. He doesn't need Timken any more than Timken needs him. Or his money."

Reginald nodded, thinking of the Sedition Army's Boom Stick weapons, their armor, and the extensive remodeling that was being done to the Vampire Council building. It was Claude's money that was funding it all.

With a cold and dawning certainty, Reginald looked at the others and said, "We're not just looking at a takeover. We're looking at war. We're looking at genocide."

Nikki put her head in her hands. Maurice looked into the corner, avoiding the eyes of the others, as if it were his fault for having a brother.

"*If* Timken wins this election," Reginald added.

Maurice looked back over and shook his head. "I have five percent of the voter support," he said. "In no universe could I take this election from Timken."

"True," said Reginald. "But I wasn't thinking of you."

Nikki's head came up. There was murder in her eyes.

"Don't say it," she hissed.

"We have to back Charles and Walker," he said.

The idea of throwing their support behind Charles, as repugnant as it was, fell apart exactly three seconds later when Maurice pointed out that none of them had any support to give. Maurice volunteered to record a video in which he made a passionate case for Charles's candidacy, but even if it was one hundred percent effective (which it wouldn't be), the most he could swing into Charles's camp would be five percent. And after tonight's performance at the speeches, Timken would already command well over half of the voters, — maybe closer to sixty percent. It wouldn't make any difference. Reginald had nothing to give, and nobody even knew who Nikki was.

Nikki, with a bona-fide "Eureka!" then suggested blowing the whistle on Timken and Claude rather than supporting their opposition. It had all of the joys of bringing down the very bad man without the oily feel of propping up the slightly less bad man. Maurice could tell the world what he'd just told them, and the people could decide for themselves. But Reginald shook his head.

"Two big problems there," he said. "For one, there's no proof. Timken is the hero who caught those responsible for the TGV tragedy and repaired human/vampire relations. All we have are four eyewitness accounts putting Claude on the scene, but it's our word against theirs. And right here, right now, if the hated ex-Deacon here —" He slapped Maurice's shoulder with the back of his hand. "— and his inferior, almost-executed sidekick —" Reginald stuck his thumb in his own chest. "— suddenly accuse the hero of wrongdoing based solely on something they claim to have seen and that nobody else saw, what do you think will happen?"

Nikki closed her eyes and shook her head.

"The second problem — the bigger problem," he went on, "is that the Vampire Nation is walking on glass right now. This election — our first — *has* to be a success. Here's another hypothetical for you: What do you think would happen if humans heard that the US Vampire Nation's heir-apparent was responsible for the biggest rail disaster ever and that his running mate has designs to eliminate the human race, save a handful of blood cows? It wouldn't matter that we 'discovered it in time,' even if Timken ended up in jail or dead. They'd consider it a terrifying near-miss. Remember, humans don't look at us in the same way they look at other humans. If a bad human takes power, they try to oust him and then tell themselves that most people aren't like he was. Not so for vampires. A bad vampire takes power and they'll assume it's validation that we are, in fact, all murderous savages. We're monsters to them. This would just solidify that impression. Now, for the first time, because they're seeing familiar symbols like voting and speeches and diplomacy and international cooperative taskforces and sober-looking men and women in suits, they're starting to believe that we could be like them. But that would change if they knew the truth. They'd never trust us again. They'd consider us a very real mortal threat and would immediately begin making very bad plans against us, no matter what they said on the outside."

Reginald shook his head, becoming more certain as he spoke.

"We can't sway the vote unless we tell the vampires of the world, and we can't tell the vampires of the world without the humans also somehow hearing what we're saying. No, this has to be handled quietly. We need to take this election from him in a fair fight somehow. He's got to lose, but we have to make that happen with our hands — with our biggest information bomb — tied behind our backs. We can't tell people that Timken and Claude are evil. We have to convince them that Charles and Walker are awesome."

Nikki clasped her hand over her mouth. "I think I'm going to be sick," she said. Then she ran into the bathroom.

Maurice looked at Reginald. "Or we could kill them," he said, his fangs popping out.

Reginald laughed. It felt good, having his old strategic mind back and feeling his confidence in his abilities return. "A thousand troops, he has protecting him," he said. "And he's always training more. Have you heard about his Young Seditionists group?"

Maurice nodded, already conceding the point. Of course he'd heard. Timken hand-picked the best, most high-ability members of each vampire academy's newly turned graduates and invited them into an elite group called the Young Seditionists. It was considered a huge brand of honor, on par with being tapped for Phi Beta Kappa (appealing to the intellectuals) or the Navy SEALS (appealing to the athletes and warriors). Initiates were given a snazzy uniform and everything.

"Why does nobody find it odd that his group still thinks of itself as seditionists?" said Maurice.

"It's just become a brand name," said Reginald, shrugging to reinforce the point that vampires, like humans, tended to be stupid when making decisions as a group.

Nikki returned from the bathroom with a red-stained paper towel in her hand. "It's bad," she said. "Now I'm vomiting blood."

So they found themselves back at square one, faced with an impossible task: convincing tens of thousands of vampires to vote for the man they'd collectively deposed and imprisoned, instead of the man who'd saved them from chaos and restored order and calm to the Nation.

They started by telling Karl and the EU Council what they knew. Karl seemed surprisingly nonplussed. The Council was aghast and required some convincing, but that happened quickly once Karl said that he agreed with Reginald's conclusions. All of the EU Council members were old enough to know about the Annihilist movement, and the more they thought about it, it seemed convenient that all of those "responsible" for the TGV disaster had been killed. It was a little too tidy. They trusted that Maurice was telling the truth about his brother, and Karl had never really been comfortable since the first time he'd seen the Boom Sticks in action. He hadn't liked the way Timken had seized power, regardless of whether power needed to be seized. *The shock troops. The speech. Climbing onto a chair like a conqueror.* It had all rubbed him the wrong way from the first.

"Okay," said Karl. "So we kill him."

"That's your solution to everything," said a Council member named Gregory who was easily the size of Brian Nickerson. Gregory should have been intimidating, but his voice was tiny and feminine and he had a tattoo of Bugs Bunny on his calf that was always visible because Gregory always wore a huge pair of mustard-colored shorts. Gregory was the one who'd told Reginald about tattoos. Apparently tattoos were similar to scars, but not similar enough for the vampire agent to universally save them when a person turned. Gregory had had an "awesome" tattoo on his back of a clockwork woman that had vanished when he'd turned, but he was forever stuck with Bugs. It was as if something inside of him hated him and was playing a cruel joke.

"We can't kill him," said Reginald, and explained his strategic reasons why they'd never get close.

"We can try," said Karl, who often disbelieved Reginald's predictions on principle. It wasn't that he didn't trust Reginald; it was that he believed in free will and felt that Reginald's analyses contradicted it.

"Sure," said Reginald. "If you want to die." And he reminded Karl about the Boom Sticks and the armor that all of Timken's men wore.

Karl pouted, reluctantly deciding that Reginald was right and not liking it at all.

Pent up and needing to vent, Reginald even bored Claire with the dilemma during a few of their almost-nightly Skype sessions. Claire feigned interest as far as an eleven-year old could feign interest in the political machinations of a different species half a world away, which was not much. So while Reginald told her about Charles and Timken and what sounded like a thrilling door-knocking campaign that was in the offing, she amused herself by using her Merlin powers to manipulate both her Skype image and, disturbingly, the contents of Reginald's hard drive. Her nose elongated. Her mouth widened like the Cheshire cat. She took photos from Reginald's photo album, manipulated them, and showed them back to him.

"Who's this, Reginald?" she said as a photo appeared on his screen. The photo showed him standing next to the Wolfman.

"How are you doing that?" he asked.

"What?"

"Where do I start? How are you using the computer without touching it? How are you accessing *my* machine? And how are you Photoshopping these images so well? It looks like I'm actually there with him." Reginald touched the screen as he'd touch a real photo, as if to see if it was real. And as far as a collection of electronic images and light could be real, it was.

Claire shrugged as if the questions bored her.

"Do you consciously think about each step, or...?"

"Who's this, Reginald?"

The new picture showed Nikki and Reginald with SpongeBob SquarePants.

"Should we be done? Maybe we're done for the day."

The picture disappeared and again he found himself looking at Claire. She was waving both hands in surrender. "No, no," she said. "Okay, fine. I don't know how I'm doing it. Other than that I'm just *doing* it."

Reginald had watched her abilities develop at a frightening speed. He'd seen kids click with new abilities before; he had a nephew who, after weeks of failing to even stand erect on downhill skis, had one day begun skiing intermediate slopes at high speeds and executing perfect turns. But Claire didn't just click with her new abilities. She clicked on top of the clicks she's already clicked. Last week she'd figured out that she could access Reginald's hard drive, and he'd luckily had time to get all of the sex videos that Nikki had wanted to take safely onto a thumb drive before she'd found them. But then within a few more days, here she was, manipulating images like a pro. Next week she'd be editing random audio into masterpieces.

"What do you mean, you're 'just doing it'?"

"I just think it." She shrugged. "Like... watch."

Reginald watched the photo of himself next to SpongeBob. In front of his eyes, SpongeBob turned from yellow to blue.

"Do *you* know how I might be doing it?" she asked.

Reginald shook his head. "This is new ground as far as I can tell. But ultimately all of this —" He tapped the computer, causing his video image to shake. "— is just energy. You're pushing around electrons."

"And the whole 'seeing the future' thing? My knowing about your train crash half a world away?"

"There's a lot we don't know about energy in the world," he said, deciding not to bore her by telling her about quantum entanglement and faster-than-light particles that seemed to be moving backward in time.

Claire made a resigned little frown, as if she'd gotten tired of talking about it.

Watching her, an idea flitted into Reginald's mind. Then, like one of those quantum particles he'd just been pondering, it vanished, leaving nothing but uncertainty. He had a sensation of a near miss, as if Claire had almost solved a problem for him without even meaning to. But he couldn't grasp it, and so he told her goodnight and let it go.

Over the following night, Reginald and Karl tried to brainstorm ways to assist Charles's campaign. It felt like wasted time, and Reginald wanted to give up and order a pizza. They compromised by ordering a pizza *while* wasting the time. Then, when the buzzer at the Chateau's side door buzzed, Karl ran up the stairs before Reginald could, through the hidden door in the back of the Chateau's Cave, and up through the empty school to the door to the outside. He returned with Reginald's pizza in one hand and the pizza man's hand in the other.

The pizza man seemed to be an American on exchange. He had long, stringy blonde hair that had been tied back into an untidy ponytail and sported a nervous, impatient expression.

"This place seems earthy," he said to Reginald, looking around with approval. "Do you sprout your own beans down here?"

That didn't make sense to Reginald, but the kid already looked pale and strung out and was jerking his head around like a bird on speed, tapping his foot and slapping his hand rapidly against his leg. Reginald had seen massive blood loss drive people into one of two extremes — sedate and drugged, or a fight-or-flight kind of mania, as the body fought its torpor with adrenaline.

Karl offered him a seat next to Reginald.

"You're keeping him?" said Reginald. "He doesn't look like he can take any more."

"I have not bitten him yet," said Karl, still gesturing toward the chair. The kid refused to sit.

"Oh. Well, he just seems so keyed up from..."

"I haven't glamoured him yet, either," Karl said, interrupting him.

"So you guys are vampires?" said the pizza man, looking at Karl's fangs. "That's cool. Blood comes from the body. There are no additives or preservatives. You can't get any healthier than blood."

Reginald looked at Karl. Karl looked at the kid's neck.

"You could have fed outside," said Reginald, wanting to chastise Karl but unable since the Chateau was, essentially, his own house.

"My dog is a vegan," said the kid.

Reginald didn't know how to reply to that. So he offered the kid a drink.

"Okay," said the kid.

"We have pop, wine, water..."

"Whatever's healthiest," the kid interrupted him.

Karl brushed a few loose hairs off of the pizza man's neck, moved his face closer, and inhaled slowly.

"... gasoline..." Reginald continued.

"Whatever's healthiest."

That's when Karl bit him. Blood welled under his lower lip, then spilled to the kid's clavicle. The sight of Karl feeding made Reginald want to feed as well. So he leaned forward on the pizza man's other side, reached over his shoulder, and removed two pieces of pizza from the box. Then he sandwiched them cheese-to-cheese and began to devour the whole works like a sandwich.

It was as if the kid didn't realize someone had bitten his neck. His eyes followed Reginald, whose fangs were out and making holes in the pizza sandwich like a cashier punching a Sub Club card.

"I don't think it's healthy for a vampire to eat pizza," the kid scolded.

Reginald dipped the tip of his pizza sandwich in the pool of blood that had formed in the hollow at the kid's clavicle, then held the red-tipped pizza up in demonstration before taking a bite.

"My dog is a vegan," the kid repeated while Karl made sucking noises at his neck that sounded like someone who's reached the bottom of a cup with a straw.

The fact that Karl had brought the kid down seemed to indicate that Karl wanted to eat while strategizing as Reginald had planned to do with his pizza, but the kid had large bug eyes that wouldn't stop staring at him, seeming to judge him for his unhealthy vampire habits. They were like the eyes on a magical painting. They seemed to follow him around the room. He thought about glamouring the kid to make him stop, but he didn't want to look into those eyes. He wanted to let Karl deal with it. He was the one who'd made the mess.

Because Reginald refused to talk shop with the kid watching him, Karl rolled his own eyes in frustration, took a final drink, and led the kid upstairs. When he returned, he reported that he'd glamoured the kid but that the kid had initially refused to leave because he seemed to suspect that Karl might have weed. So Karl had pulled a handful of grass from the lawn and had handed it to the kid, who'd run off with it tucked in his palm like a secret.

"Remind me why we want to stop Maurice's brother from killing all of the humans?" Karl said as he descended the large stone staircase.

Then they got down to business, but the arrival of a pizza hadn't made the effort feel any less futile. The election was in less than two weeks and sentiment had shifted even more firmly toward Timken. Informal Fangbook polls showed that Timken commanded fifty-eight percent of the vote and that Charles's percentage had dropped to nineteen. Maurice was holding firm at five percent. The only reason he hadn't formally removed himself from the ballot was a conviction that doing so would swing the entirety of that five percent to Timken, no matter what he told his supporters in his concession statement. If the polls were exact predictors, which they weren't, that left eighteen percent undecided. Even in the best-case scenario, eighteen percent undecided plus nineteen percent for Charles was still less than two-thirds of what Timken commanded.

Hours and hours passed. Nikki came and went. Maurice came and went. Reginald finished the pizza by himself. They both did several caffeine-spiked blood shots — Karl because he wanted the pick-me-up and Reginald because he barely consumed more blood as a vampire than he had protein as a human, and both dietary habits were equally destructive. They made notes and opened folders stuffed with paper. They made charts. They wore out Google trying to search for ways to help themselves win an election, but there seemed to be no way to make it work. They couldn't make Charles look good enough in time, and they couldn't make Timken look bad enough to bring him down without inviting very serious side effects from the humans. Timken was going to win the election, and there was nothing they could do about it.

"Let's kill him," said Karl.

Reginald didn't respond. Karl had suggested killing Timken every half hour for the entire night, and by now it was simply a form of verbal masturbation for him. They couldn't remove Timken by force. They couldn't make him lose the election. They couldn't disrupt the election, either, which was another of Karl's frequent suggestions. "If you can't win the game, change the rules," he said, but Reginald kept insisting that as much as he believed in bending rules, this was one contest that had to be won by the book because the book was the game itself. The election process had to be legitimized, both to calm an already panicky vampire population and to show itchy-trigger-fingered humans that they could behave like civilized beings rather than the monsters that humans — and their well-armed AVT forces — were convinced they were.

"Should we contact Charles?" said Reginald. "Coordinate efforts?"

But there was nothing to coordinate. Charles was an insufferable idiot, and Walker was a charismatic idiot. Neither insufferability nor charisma won contests by themselves, and it was painfully obvious that neither Charles nor Walker had any clue as to what they were doing. Timken, in a publicly-lauded act of generosity and fairness, had even freed Charles from custody because he said that a fair election couldn't be conducted with one man in a cage. Charles was watched but otherwise free, and still he couldn't rally support. Everything he did made him look worse — or, in Reginald's opinion, made it obvious just what a total and completely dangerous asshole he actually was.

"Let's kill him," said Karl.

It was a joke, but Reginald stopped to consider it. He'd thrown out the box when it had become apparent that their only chance was to think incredibly far outside of it. What would happen if Charles died suddenly? But it was no use. If they framed Timken for Charles's murder, it would do nearly as much damage as revealing the truth about Timken and the TGVs. And if Charles died in another way, his absence in the election would simply make the vote unanimous.

But would it make the election a farce, and force them to hold it again? Reginald asked himself.

No, he thought. *But even if it did, how would that change the outcome?*

Timken had reached savior status. Barring a major scandal — which would be just as bad as his winning — nothing could sufficiently tarnish his image as to cause him to lose the election. Timken couldn't *lose,* so he'd have to *be defeated...* which became more and more impossible with each passing day.

The night ended on a depressing note. Sometime after sunrise, Karl went to bed. Reginald cleaned up the paperwork and his notes, resisted the urge to throw them away, and dropped them into a wastebasket-shaped file instead. Maybe they'd be thrown out. Maybe they wouldn't. It didn't matter.

He talked it out with Nikki. Nikki didn't try to help. She

simply tried to make him feel better, but was unable. So she laid next to him, and sometime before falling asleep she slipped out of her pajamas and did what she could, without so much as punching him in the face, breaking furniture, or throwing him into a wall.

He talked it out with Maurice. Maurice didn't want to talk about it. He felt guilty. He talked about all of the signs that Claude had exhibited over the years, and said that he should have known, that he should have ended Claude when he'd had the chance. Reginald told them that all they could do would be to wait and to watch for their chance to fix things after the election. Anything was possible. And instead of Maurice making him feel better, Reginald ended up trying to do the same for Maurice.

He talked it out with Claire, but Claire didn't understand or care. She'd lived with terror in the background for months. She'd known that monsters were real for a full year. She'd more or less lived inside her house since they'd left the country, and she was becoming pale and sick-looking. It couldn't be good for her. The vampire world had, since Timken's takeover, fallen again into obscurity for Claire. She stayed inside on principle, to be safe for a while longer, but she told Reginald that the gangs of creatures that had been roaming the streets just a few weeks ago were gone. The world felt safer. She asked Reginald if maybe he was wrong. Maybe order — even a terrifying kind of order — was better than the disintegration that she'd hidden from and that her vampire friends had fled from. Maybe Timken was hungry for power, but what politician wasn't? Maybe he'd settle in and rule, and maybe he'd become like Logan and shut down democracy, and maybe he'd be a tyrant... but maybe that was how it was supposed to be, and maybe it was okay.

That was the one possibility Reginald hadn't considered. What if they simply let events unfold and allowed Timken to win? Maybe it would be like Claire said.

But as nice as the idea felt for two seconds, he couldn't make it fit. It reminded him of the time his car had been banging and clattering and then had stopped for an hour, and he'd hoped against hope that it had fixed itself. But of course it hadn't, and of course ignoring Timken wouldn't end well. Dismissing the damning evidence and expecting the return of the status-quo was too miraculous and serendipitous to be correct. Every scenario his strategic vampire mind had explored — and there were thousands of variants — ended in war and genocide. There was simply no way he could make the facts fit a peaceful mold. The irony was that war was coming... exactly as Claire had predicted back on that hill in Germany, back before she had realized it was a prediction at all.

Reginald had attached his cell phone to his laptop to download some photos, and now, out of the corner of his eye, he saw the screen of the phone brighten. He looked over and saw that his phone's desktop image had changed to one of Claire holding two thumbs up. Underneath was the message, *Don't worry, be happy*.

Then a thought occurred to him. It ran from the base of his spine up into the crown of his head, then crept through his cerebrum like fingers. Everything was on fire. Scenarios unfolded. And for a moment, there was hope.

"Hey Claire," he asked his computer screen. "Could you hack the vampire version of Facebook?"

Reginald's web browser opened and he saw his main Fangbook news feed. At the top was a new status update from a user with the screen name of SpongeBob SquarePants.

The status update read, *Of course I could.*

MAGIC FINGERS

Claire was being somewhat overconfident, but not much.

Over the week that followed, she explored the Fangbook network using Reginald's login, which Claire, on her own, thought to spoof so that he appeared to be logging in from Europe so as not to alert any unwanted attention. Reginald didn't give her his password; she simply thought her way in. She then proceeded to post photos which she'd cobbled together from her memory, from her creative subconscious, or from nothing: Reginald by the leaning tower of Pisa, which he'd never visited; Reginald standing on the bank of a Venice canal next to a man he'd never met; Reginald and Nikki and Maurice giving noogies to a wax museum figure of Margaret Thatcher, which they'd never done. At first, Reginald asked how she was creating the images, but after enough vague, disinterested, *well-duh* answers involving imagining pictures in the same way she'd think a thought, he stopped asking.

Claire reported that she was getting more and more comfortable with the process every day. She said that it felt like swimming. *Swimming*, Reginald said to Nikki, baffled. It wasn't like looking at a screen and changing things in the way she used to do with a keyboard or a mouse. It was more like she entered the data itself and simply pushed it around. Encryption didn't bother her in the least. She demonstrated that she could transfer money back and forth between Reginald's bank and Nikki's without credentials or an EFT authorization. She bought Nikki flowers using Reginald's credit card because she said that Reginald was almost certainly not appreciating Nikki enough. She added a period in an obscure place in a *New York Times* online article so as not to attract notice, just to prove that she could do it. She asked Reginald if she could change the front page of CNN to read "Go Browns," but Reginald objected on the basis of both the attention it would draw and the fact that he didn't like the Cleveland Browns at all.

Then, focusing in on the task at hand, Claire tried manipulating inconsequential Fangbook votes. A minor measure was placed in front of the populous by the reestablished Council a week before the election that altered training requirements in vampire bootcamp. Claire read and announced the results in the middle of the voting period, then toggled thousands of votes like little switches, changing them from no to yes... and the measure, which was going to fail, passed with flying colors.

Timken had promised that the Fangbook election system was drum tight and unhackable. Reginald searched the internet and made phone calls and read everything he could about it. He even tried to hack it for hours on end, and got nowhere. After all of his research and investigation, Reginald was eventually able to determine two things: first, although Timken had commissioned the election-specific additions to the system as well as bankrolled and championed it, it seemed that he did not, in fact, have any sort of back door access to it. And second, the system was indeed impossible to hack... except, apparently, by a young girl who didn't need a key to get through any electronic door.

The election security issue had been pored over from dozens of distinct and independent directions. Timken had rightly assumed that people would be suspicious about a system that wielded so much power and its ability to be influenced — either in software or via plain old corruption — by any person, and specifically by the person who had pushed and funded it. Timken had gone out of his way to provide everything that skeptics would need to assuage their doubts. The lengths to which Timken had gone to assure the public that the election would be fair was, in itself, suspicious to Reginald. It had the feel of a magician who draws attention with one hand so that the audience won't watch the other hand working under the table. It led Reginald to believe that the Fangbook system was indeed straight and fair, because it was the shown hand. The decoy *had* to be imperturbable and unassailable. So where was the other hand — the one that was performing the tricks?

But of course, there *was* no hidden hand. Timken didn't need an ace up his sleeve because he was playing fair. It was *Reginald* who was cheating.

Still, Reginald pursued every angle he could conceive of — every way that Timken might be able to influence the vote's outcome. He'd determined that the system was fair, but what about access to the data? Were there vulnerabilities with Fangbook itself? Was it possible for a network of hackers to intervene between individual voters and the system, closer to their points of access, which were less secure? Could a virus be distributed in advance of the election that could act on an individual computer's level, casting votes for Timken regardless of what the user entered or saw on her screen? What about the vampires that were involved? Did those higher up at Fangbook have sufficient access to cause problems, and could they be bought? Could the voters themselves be influenced or persuaded or threatened? Could a person other than a given voter cast a vote for that person?

But no matter how Reginald looked at it and no matter how paranoid he was and no matter how many permutations his super-brain ran through, he could find no weaknesses beyond infinitesimal issues that would never make more than infinitesimal differences in the outcome. The election would be fair. And that was, in one sense, good news. But in another sense, it was troubling news. If there was no known way to perturb the outcome of the election, how could one eleven-year-old girl do it?

"Magic fingers," said Claire in a *fuhgeddaboutit* tone of voice when Reginald expressed his concerns. Then she wiggled her fingers in front of her camera and Reginald watched as blue arcs of electricity jumped between her fingers like sparks from a Van de Graaff generator.

"When did that start happening?" said Reginald, shocked. So far, he hadn't even been thinking of what Claire could do as magic because there had been no visible phenomena. He realized he'd been thinking of it more like computer hacking, though it seemed far more creative and far more powerful.

"It didn't," said Claire. "I just made your video do it."

Reginald sighed. "Could you not do that? I'm starting to doubt my reality. I kind of need to know that what I see is real. You've totally destroyed the truth of 'seeing is believing' for me."

"Sorry. Sure."

"You promise?"

"Yeah," she said. "I promise. I keep my promises."

Then something occurred to him. Wasn't she pushing electrons right now?

"Have you tried other stuff?" he asked. "Stuff that looks all..."

"Like stuff a wizard would do?" she said.

"I guess."

"Like appearing on the side of a van beside a woman in a bikini and a tiger's head, possibly holding a laser gun that goes 'ZAP!'?"

"Um..."

"The answer is yes," said Claire, laughing. "What little girl doesn't want to be able to shoot lightning bolts and read crystal balls? But so far, zilch. But that would be bad ass."

"*Claire*," Reginald said in a scolding tone.

"Sorry. That would be *awesome*, I mean."

Reginald thought to have her try a few things while he watched, but there would be time for that later, after the election. He bet himself a dozen donuts that she would eventually to be able to do things like her video image had just shown. She'd probably be able to control thoughts, too. It was all just energy. And as a plus, even if he was wrong, he'd win a dozen donuts.

"But to my original point," he said. "The election software is different from what's been used for the smaller Fangbook votes so far. It isn't native to Fangbook. It's open to scrutiny but is very black box once you're under the hood. There will be no way to determine if you can hack it until it's up and running. Without data in it, it's just encryption."

"Your silly encryption is nothing to one as powerful as me," said Claire with a mad scientist's laugh.

"You don't know that."

"Sure I do. Let me at it. Let me see right now if I can get inside it."

"Getting inside doesn't prove that you'll be able to influence a live data set," said Reginald. "It's complicated."

"You mean that you don't think I'll understand it."

"I didn't mean that. But also yes. I don't think you'll be able to understand it, because I don't. It doesn't use encryption keys. I don't see how that's possible, and I'm super awesome."

"What are encryption keys?" said Claire.

"I told you that you wouldn't be able to understand it," said Reginald.

A spark jumped from Reginald's keyboard to his finger, making him jump. It was a tiny thing, no more than a static shock.

"I don't have to understand it to do it," said Claire.

But despite Claire's confidence, Reginald, Nikki, Maurice, and Karl remained skeptical and nervous. None of the rest of the EU

Council knew of the plan because 1) it was highly, highly illegal, bordering on treason, and 2) it seemed prudent to minimize the potential security leaks behind the whole operation. Karl didn't believe any of it was remotely possible. Nikki was guardedly optimistic but unconvinced. Maurice was mostly apathetic, and Reginald was a basket case.

Six days before the election, the impartial committee in charge of the election announced that all voters would be required to reconfirm their identity via a genetic scan. This introduced an entire new level of difficulty and set off alarm bells in Reginald's head. Claire would no longer be required just to manipulate a simple pool of votes once past the security. The committee had distributed devices that took a finger-stick blood sample before opening a two-minute voting window for an individual voter. Reginald knew nothing about the technology. It must electronically assay for a genetic fingerprint that was unique from person to person, but which sequence did they use? There was no way that the system was storing each voter's entire genetic sequence. That wasn't possible... but then, neither was encryption that didn't use encryption keys. And what, then, did the system do with that data? Did it store the sample data beside the vote... and if so, was it time-stamped? Would Claire's manipulations change those timestamps? Would the addition of a whole new genetic sample table (or series of tables) affect her ability to change the votes? And if it did, how could she possibly manage that much interconnected data?

"Breathe," Claire told Reginald. "I keep telling you, this isn't about moving numbers around. This is *magic*."

"What does *that* mean?" said Reginald, not at all mollified.

"It means that it's like dreaming. Do you build every element of a dream? Or do you have a full, very-real-at-the-time dream experience that you don't question because your subconscious mind knows what it's doing?"

"This isn't making me feel better."

"Reginald, I can create a video right now of you skateboarding with Gerald Ford. Do you really think I'm such an excellent artist that I know where to put those billions of pixels? Or do you think that either my subconscious mind or something outside of me might be taking the *spirit* of my intention and handling the details for me?"

"Make your fingers spark," said Reginald.

Onscreen, the small girl with the charming smile snapped her fingers and there was a bright white flash, like a photo strobe.

"Did you do that for real, or was it a video effect?"

"I keep my promises," she said.

Reginald couldn't quiet his gut, so he fed it. He couldn't quiet his mind, so Nikki fed Reginald's gut, this time with nourishing blood. And ultimately, Maurice's apathy convinced both of them that there was no point in driving themselves insane with worry. It would either work or it wouldn't, and if it *didn't* work, that was no worse than having never tried. So with an attitude of *que sera, sera* (which Karl informed him wasn't even correct syntax), Reginald sat down in front of his computer on election day and waited to watch the future of the world.

He didn't need to worry. For most of the day, Claire did nothing and Reginald heard nothing from her. The polls closed at noon GMT, and until 11am GMT, Reginald simply watched election coverage and fretted with Nikki beside him. Then a little after eleven, Claire Skyped him and informed him that Charles Barkley was now leading the election by six percent — just enough to win without being obvious, as Reginald had requested. Reginald asked if she was sure. She rolled her eyes. Reginald asked if it had been difficult. Claire rolled her eyes again, and at the same time, a video appeared on Reginald's computer screen beside the Skype window. It showed Reginald skateboarding with Gerald Ford.

Nikki's face scrunched as she peered at the screen.

"I thought he was dead," she said.

"Well, so am I," said Reginald.

Reginald, assurances and skateboarding videos with Gerald Ford aside, was unconvinced. Claire had been projecting her interpretation of the aggregate data into his computer screen all day, and he said that he hadn't seen it tick up in Barkley's favor. Claire told him that he was looking at the wrong data set, and with that, the window showing the Fangbook data changed. And he saw that indeed, Barkley was leading. But only by five percent.

"They really like the other guy, so new votes have already closed the gap on what I just did," said Claire. "I'll tweak it again as it gets closer to ending."

The next hour passed without incident. At midnight GMT, coverage announced that polls were closed and that the counting had begun. But Reginald already had the results in front of him. Former Councilman Charles Barkley had captured forty-seven percent of the vote. Nicholas Timken had fallen short, at forty-three percent.

Reginald had ten minutes to meditate on what he'd just done — what kind of a future the Vampire Nation and the world was in for under Barkley — before the door at the top of the cathedral room staircase exploded inward and a flood of Sedition Army troops rushed in with their Boom Sticks drawn.

BUSTED

Reginald looked up, jumped, and backed against the wall. Nikki was beside him; she flinched forward to fight but he held her by the arm, as hard as he could, until she looked over and saw his wide eyes and stopped struggling.

Councilman Mellus was coming up from the lower catacombs when the rubble from the door began to rattle down the steps and, seeing the intruders, rushed at them without thinking. The soldier in front raised the Boom Stick he was carrying. There was a bright blue spark a snapping noise and Mellus disintegrated instantly into ash, billowing upward in a surprised cloud and then settling down as if someone had just pulled a rug out from under it. Then several others — Lola, who'd seduced the angel Santos, the eternally pregnant Greta, a man Reginald barely knew named Harmon, others — blurred like lightning into the room, having heard the explosion. The stood ready with hands hooked into claws, their fangs out. They advanced toward the shock troops as if they hadn't realized what the armored soldiers were carrying.

There was a blur and Karl appeared in front of the group, facing the troops, his arms wide, his palms facing backward. He pushed them back, repeating over and over not to engage, to stand down, as if the vampires of the Chateau were the soldiers. And still the Sedition Army advanced. They moved like humans, slowly, their red helmets' blank visors scanning their opposition, sizing them up. They also moved like military; one walked forward, stopping at the bottom of the stairs with his weapon out and then motioning for the others to walk down and join him.

More vampires spilled up from the lower tunnels, having been drawn by the noise. The troops faced them, Karl urgently repeating their every order: *Get back. Don't move.*

Reginald hadn't moved from his computer. He still gripped Nikki's arm tight enough to leave a mark (until she healed, anyway) and he still stood dead still, his brain processing it all, categorizing, analyzing their chances. But this wasn't like the American Council escape. These weren't vampires fighting with their hands and teeth. These were trained troops with weapons. It wouldn't matter whether Reginald could appear to slow time or push away pain. It wouldn't matter how fast the Chateau vampires could move or how well he could direct them. The twitch of one finger on any of the red-helmeted men would end them with a shard of silver through the heart.

There was movement behind Karl, and Reginald realized that Maurice was pushing his way through from the back of the crowd. His mind reached a lightning-fast conclusion: Maurice was the only new arrival to the siege who knew what they'd done, why the troops were here, and what it was all likely to mean. Maurice's movements said that he was miliseconds away from fighting for his life. He either hadn't yet noticed their Boom Sticks or thought he could outmaneuver them.

Once he was past the crowd, Maurice was going to attack. And then he was going to die.

Reginald and Nikki were against a wall very near the entrance to the catacombs, closer to Maurice than Maurice was to the soldiers. Reginald felt a twitch in his grip as Nikki wrenched herself free. Maurice cleared the crowd and leaped at the same time Nikki did. They met in the air, Nikki taking Maurice around the waist like a flying tackle. They slammed to the ground in the corner, still safely back from the troops, who twitched forward and pointed their weapons. Nikki and Maurice flipped over. They flipped over again, now with Nikki on top. She wasn't a tenth as strong as he was, but she was on top with his hands pinned, and something in her face must have caused things to click for Maurice. All of the tension went out of his body. Then it was over, and Nikki got up and released him, and Maurice nodded something to her that looked like a thank-you. Both of them returned to Reginald's side. The invading soldiers watched it all happen, only vaguely interested, their Boom Sticks held out like microphones.

The soldier in the lead pulled off his helmet. He was a young-looking vampire with a head of wavy blonde hair and a narrow, hawklike face. He holstered his Boom Stick. Then, with a look but no word, he walked over to Reginald, flanked by two others who hadn't removed their helmets or holstered their weapons.

The man looked at Reginald, then at the screen of his computer. The monitoring window that showed the election data was still open in the center, green text visible on a black background.

The blonde man looked back up at Reginald and gave him a look that was strange; it was almost as if the man, who Reginald didn't know, was disappointed in him.

Wearing gloves, the soldier removed a pair of silver handcuffs from a pouch on his belt and said, "Reginald Baskin, you are under arrest for treason, as an enemy of the Sovereign American Vampire Nation."

"As a seditionist?" said Maurice from behind Reginald.

Keeping his eyes on Maurice, the soldier closed the cuffs on Reginald's wrists.

Reginald looked out the window of the plane. Below him, the Atlantic ocean looked black and bottomless, an endless void pocked only by a few pinprick lights from freighters.

The blonde soldier was beside him, now wearing civilian clothes. Beside the blonde man, in the aisle seat, was another vampire Reginald didn't know. He had a solid, no-nonsense build and wore a solid, no-nonsense black haircut. This one's name was Rolf. The blonde man was Tim. Rolf was German and Tim was American. They were a perfect example of the new spirit of international cooperation. And, by virtue of the full permission that the vampires had to transport a prisoner overseas on a human airliner, it was a perfect example of inter*species* cooperation. Reginald stared at the sliver handcuffs on his wrists, which were resting in his lap. Everyone was working together happily, all in agreement that the folks in the Chateau de Differdange needed to be quelled. If Reginald were in anyone else's shoes, he'd think that he was the bad guy here.

He wondered if he maybe *was* the bad guy.

Having a vampire-enhanced brain gave Reginald plenty of computing power, but that big brain sometimes got restless, and sometimes it needed an idea to mull in the way his belly sometimes needed food. So, once, when his brain had been restless, Reginald had found himself pondering the ideas of sanity versus insanity. During that session, he'd decided that what was considered "sane" was nothing more than the majority opinion. Right now, most people didn't believe that ghosts plagued them at night... but if eighty percent of the population decided that ghosts were everywhere, it would be the skeptic who would find himself locked up and considered nuts. If you were in the majority, you were sane. If you were in the majority, you were normal. It was nothing more than percentages.

Reginald, Nikki, Maurice, and Karl had attempted to rig the election because they were convinced that the world was going to hell. It made sense to them, but most of the world thought the world was going in the correct direction. So in this instance, how were *they* not the insane ones?

People don't know the truth about Timken and Claude, Reginald thought. *If they knew the truth, they'd see that we were doing the right thing.*

But that was probably what a man who kills his neighbor because he thinks he's Satan would say, too.

Reginald alone was being transported back to America. The Chateau was being occupied and watched — a kind of wholesale house arrest, during which none of them would be allowed to leave — but only Reginald had been speed-extradited. And why not? He was the only one that Tim had an arrest warrant for. Maurice had even held his wrists up for the cuffs, but Tim had waved him away, saying, "You are not under arrest here, Deacon Toussant." Nikki had begged to go. She'd given an impromptu confession. She'd offered to pay for her own plane ticket on the red-eye to New York. But short of attacking the soldiers, there was nothing she could do to convince them. So Reginald had said his goodbyes and they'd led him away, leaving shocked, defeated faces behind him.

The flight staff thought that Rolf and Tim were CIA agents. Both carried human firearms and badges. The human authorities, with permission going all the way up to Erickson's office, had given them the guns and stars.

Rolf didn't speak English very well, but once his armor and Boom Stick had been put away (either one of the faux agents could easily subdue Reginald without a weapon), Tim had turned out to be very talkative. He'd been quite cordial to Reginald. Their business had been concluded for the time being; Reginald was in cuffs and, before sunrise, would be in a cell in New York. The next night he'd be transferred to the formal Council cells at the new and improved facility under the Asbury Club in Columbus. Tim seemed to have decided that there was no reason for further acrimony. Tim had won; the Council had won; Timken had won; Reginald and his rebel cause had lost. They'd been discovered and the election would be held again. So Tim and Rolf and Reginald could play out the whole coppers-with-a-grudge-and-angry-prisoner thing, or they could be three people on a plane with 24 hours or more together in front of them.

Reginald, who wasn't a spiteful type anyway, was happy to pretend he wasn't wearing cuffs and that the soldiers wouldn't be tasked with killing him (and quite able to do so) if he tried to escape. And so they talked, like men.

Reginald was curious how the troops had found him and discovered their ruse. There was no reason for secrecy, so Tim told him what he knew. Because the election process was so new and because Timken wanted it to go as fairly as possible and be conducted in the way that gave the public as much faith in it as possible, twelve independent watchdogs in twelve different locations and representing twelve different groups had been watching aggregate election data as it came in. They couldn't watch the vote tallies or see who was leading and they couldn't watch demographics, but they could see the trends — which party was rallying and which was flagging, what the relative ratios between any two candidates' votes were over time. Watchdogs were isolated and were not allowed to communicate with the outside world during the day of the election and were required to submit their own votes in advance.

When every one of the watchdogs reported a sudden spike in one candidate's votes and a corresponding dip in the other's votes, word had quickly been sent up the chain of command.

Reginald shook his head when Tim told him this part. It made sense that they'd be able to see a dramatic spike corresponding to a certain time. In hindsight, it was obvious that he should have had Claire change votes slowly, throughout the course of the day. It would have required much more work in order to make it convincing, but what they'd done had been a very obvious mistake. He was supposed to be a mastermind. It was all his fault.

Timken, Tim said, had warned his corporals about Reginald from the very beginning. Reginald, sitting in the plane, couldn't help but feel flattered. He'd only met Timken briefly that one time on Skype, but apparently Reginald's reputation preceded him. Maurice was considered a physical threat and a disruptive influence, but word about Reginald's incredible mental prowess had become legend. *Was it true he'd hacked the old Council relocation algorithm?* Tim had asked him. *Yes*, Reginald had replied. And Tim had actually whistled and smiled, impressed.

So from the beginning and through the election process, Timken had considered Reginald to be a threat to the democratic process of the Vampire Nation as sure as a vulnerability in the election system itself would be a threat. Timken's men had watched key areas for evidence of corruption. They'd distributed early access to the election software to independent authorities who would verify and monitor its fairness. And they'd kept an eye on Reginald Baskin. They'd known exactly where he was. Reginald had been none too choosy about where he used his credit card, and Timken, unlike Charles, had the intelligence and the wherewithal to use it to track him.

"Apparently you were logging into Fangbook from a local Luxembourg ISP, too," said Tim, chucking him on the arm. "Probably should have spoofed it, huh?" And he laughed.

But of course, it *had* been spoofed, because Claire had been the one using Reginald's Fangbook login most of the time. She'd spoofed it to look like the mistake that had gotten him caught. But just the same as with Reginald's credit card, there had been no real need to be careful at first. They'd fled from Charles, whose regime was immersed in chaos and unable to track such things, and Timken wasn't a threat until it was too late.

From there, it was easy. There was one and only one obvious place in Luxembourg that Reginald and Maurice could be, Tim said.

"You knew I'd be with Karl Stromm, who was apparently a big enough threat for Timken to kill," said Reginald. It was his way of simultaneously drawing attention to the fact that he wasn't the wrong one here and also asking why the troops hadn't stormed the Chateau weeks ago.

Tim's eyebrows drew together. "What?"

"He tried to kill Karl once already. So if I was such a threat, why not burst in and kill us all, getting Karl in the bargain?"

"When did Timken try to kill Stromm?"

"The TGV disaster." And then Reginald, because there was no point in holding back, told Tim about what he'd seen and what he'd deduced.

"I know Claude," said Tim, his eyes darkening.

"And?"

"He's a bastard. You should tell Timken what you just told me when you see him."

"Tell Timken?" said Reginald. And then he realized what Tim was saying: Reginald needed to inform Timken that the his running mate had crashed the TGVs and ended untold numbers of human lives and the life of at least one vampire Deacon.

"Timken was *behind* it," Reginald said.

Tim laughed. "You sound like a conspiracy theorist."

But the difference between Reginald and a wacko conspiracy theorist was that, in this case, the conspiracy was real. Although, that was exactly what all of the wacko conspiracy theorists said, too.

There had been three TGVs that had crashed. A second vampire leader had been killed afterward. That couldn't all have been Claude and the Annihilists, could it? The TGVs had been on their way to the Paris summit. The disruption of the summit and the loss of all those leaders had benefited Timken, hadn't it?

"Even if Claude *was* behind it, and even if it wasn't just his men and his money, which it easily could have been, that crash benefitted any vampire leader who survived it," said Tim. "*Including* your man Karl."

But the implication that Karl could be to blame was absurd. Claude had walked through the train looking for Karl so that he could kill him. Reginald had heard it himself. It had been almost serendipitous, the way that sweep squad, led by Claude himself, had talked about killing Karl right under where Reginald was trapped. Right where the passenger manifest placed him. Right where Claude found him later, when Reginald had glamoured him.

Reginald shook the thought away.

"Besides," said Tim, "we're not executioners. That's for the courts to decide."

His mind was suddenly full of unwelcome doubts. It had seemed so painfully, obviously clear that Timken was in league with Claude in the TGV incident, but now he was having trouble putting the pieces together. Did he know of any direct and damning connection between Claude and Timken? He knew of a connection between Claude and Maurice, and he knew of a connection between Timken and Karl, but other than the fact that Timken had chosen Claude as his running mate, he didn't have any proof that they'd been in league when the trains had derailed.

But *Timken* was the man with the gun. *Timken* was the man who'd staged a coup. *Timken* was the one who commanded six hundred troops that had swelled to over a thousand. *Timken* was the one who was siphoning new vampires straight out of orientation and into the Young Seditionists. It was all so obvious.

Reginald looked out the window into the night, then down at the silver handcuffs around his wrists.

Anyway, Tim had explained, the very fact that Reginald's ID had been so active on Fangbook had in itself been curious. Reginald used to never use Fangbook, and now he was all over it. So when the watchdogs had reported the spike to Timken, Timken had made a phone call. The man on the other end of the phone had already been prepared, was already ready. And the rest was history.

The plane landed in New York and, thanks to a bit more human/vampire cooperation (proceeding swimmingly these days, that was), Reginald found himself spending the day in a holding cell in JFK airport while the sound of tens of thousands of human airline passengers marched by outside, disrupting his sleep. Tim didn't sleep either, and neither did Rolf.

Instead, they opened a laptop and logged in to a vampire news site. Reginald, unable to sleep across the room, was able to see the screen, and watched himself being caught red-handed during the raid as filmed through Tim's helmet camera, the fat vampire's hands up and his face ugly with guilt.

VAMPIRE SPOCK

Reginald sat in the stark white holding cell, feeling deja vu.

The now-permanent holding area of the Council structure hadn't changed during Timken's remodeling project. Reginald felt a flash back to a year ago, seeing himself as he was back when he was first turned, facing execution for being an inferior representative of his race. The white walls were the same. The silver bars were the same. The disorientation — the feeling that he didn't know which way was up because everything was smooth and white and featureless — was the same.

Again, Reginald was the prisoner. The only change was that this time, it almost felt as if he'd done something wrong, and perhaps even deserved to be here.

The one addition to the holding area was a television, which had been mounted in a corner near the ceiling. It couldn't be a true television, of course, because it was broadcasting vampire news, so it had to actually be a fullscreen feed off of a vampire news site. It seemed to repeat on an hour-long cycle. Stories had changed a few times throughout the eight cycles Reginald had seen — breaking news added as older news filtered out. The election scandal hadn't moved and had been featured in full each cycle, with new bits added each time as new events came to light.

The American Vampire Nation election had been disrupted by a group of sophisticated hackers. The method that this insurgent group had used to hack the supposedly unhackable system was, as of now, still unclear. However, the population should be assured by the fact that secondary safeguards had detected the fraud in time, though authorities were not divulging the methods through which they'd determined that the results were being tampered with. The group was led by Reginald Baskin, who became famous as an aide to Maurice Toussant, the former Deacon who'd seized power in a coup when...

The sights and sounds droned through Reginald's mind in a neverending haze. The loop repeated, and it was like going back in time. Again he was arrested, his hands in the air, a damning hacker's laptop on the desk in front of him. Again he was escorted from the Chateau de Differdange in the quaint European country of Luxembourg, which was home to the European Union's Vampire Council. Others — such as former Deacon Maurice Toussant and EU Deacon Karl Stromm — had not been implicated in the crime and were, as yet, considered innocent of wrongdoing.

That part was probably a little bit of PR bullshit, Reginald thought. Timken had to know that Karl and Maurice had been involved, but how would it look if the European head were declared a criminal?

The election's votes had been discarded, the news report continued, and the election would be repeated in two weeks' time after passing a particularly demanding new security screening. Authorities were confident that with the Baskin out of the way, the next election would go smoothly and fairly.

Cut to a clip of Timken, who expressed disappointment but remained optimistic about the future of the Vampire Nation and its citizens.

"Such pomp and circumstance, don't you agree?" said a voice.

Reginald looked over. It was Timken, who had just entered the holding area through the side door. He strolled across the room beyond the bars of Reginald's cell wearing a sober and comforting and very human-looking suit. His hair was meticulously combed and every hair was in place.

"I don't like politics," he said, reaching up and turning off the TV, "but it's what people understand. It's what the humans expect. It's what makes everyone feel quiet and comfortable. And right now, that's what we need most — comfort. It would be so easy to panic. But I watched your friend Maurice's last speech as Deacon, which I'm sure you recall word for word with that wonderful brain of yours, and he was totally right. Sometimes, the people need a lie. You're a smart man, Mr. Baskin. Don't you agree that given a choice between being bluntly truthful with the Nation about the Ring of Fire and war with the humans and their own precarious position versus being a little deceptive to maintain calm, that ultimately the deception is better?"

"You were behind the TGV crashes," said Reginald.

Timken sat on the floor, cross-legged, on the other side of the bars of Reginald's cell. "Yes."

"To consolidate power for yourself."

"For the vampires of the world."

"For yourself," Reginald repeated.

Timken made a gesture that suggested that Reginald was splitting hairs. "I'm a steward of power. I don't want it for its own sake, but I need it to do what needs to be done. Barkley was leading us into chaos and blind war and death and, possibly, right back into the sewers. The Paris summit was nice in concept, but it was just more blustering." Timken made a face that indicated his thoughts on political hot air. "What would have happened? Concessions to stay to ourselves and keep back in the shadows. Groveling, because they were angry and had the upper hand, and we were operating out of desperation. *Politicians.*" He shook his head.

"You're a politician," said Reginald.

"I'm a man who does what needs to be done," he said.

"And what needs to be done?"

Timken shifted his weight. "Logic puzzle for you, Reginald. If you could make a choice between the certain death of a few or the likely death of most, which would you choose?"

"That's not a logic puzzle," said Reginald.

Timken smiled, conceding a point won.

Realizing that Timken was still waiting for an answer, Reginald said, "I don't know."

Timken smiled and pointed at Reginald. "See?" he said. "That's my point exactly. Humans and vampires alike won't make that decision deliberately, because the only logical way to make it deliberately is to choose to let a few die. You can even do the math and determine, *in an objective way*, which is better. It's not even close. You *have* to cut your losses. You *have* to triage what you can and let the rest go. The only reasonable thing to do is to sacrifice the few to save the many, but nobody will make that choice. So they make no choice at all, which means that they default to allowing those few to live, and in the process, the inevitable happens and the majority die anyway. How much better off would they have been to choose the hard and unpopular option immediately?"

"But what if you're wrong?" said Reginald.

"And that's the trap. Say there are fifty humans in a forty-man lifeboat. Rather than forcing ten out into the water, everyone hopes that the capacity restrictions will turn out to be wrong, that the boat will defy physics and somehow stay afloat. But it can't, and all fifty die. Vampires are exactly the same, because in the beginning we were all humans, and at our cores, we still are. But it's not logical to bet on a small chance, Reginald. It's not logical to hope for the ten-percent possibility to manifest. You have to make the hard choice, in the interest of the greater good."

"What needs to be done right now?" Reginald repeated. "You took power so you could make the hard decision that others wouldn't make in order to save us all. Fine. So what's the decision?" But now that things were clicking, Reginald felt his old scenarios falling back into place. He was pretty sure he already knew the answer, and it scared him.

"This needs to become a vampire planet," said Timken. He shook his head with what looked like heavy regret. "It's the only way."

Reginald said nothing.

"You were *at* the Ring of Fire, Reginald." Timken's palms were up. He looked like he was begging. "You *know* what the angels wanted. I hear you even communed inside of their collective mind, the last time you were in Luxembourg. Look, I *like* humans. I was *raised* with humans. I've lived with them many times. I have many human friends. But what would you do in my shoes, if you take emotion out of the way and use that great logical mind of yours? Think about it! Would we have lived under Charles? Will we live if we continue to have meetings and summits and bluster and fill out forms? Logically, isn't this the only way, regrettable as it is?"

A sudden, strange thought struck Reginald like a bullet: *He brought me here to recruit me.* Then he realized that that wasn't quite right. Timken wanted his approval. He wanted Reginald to tell him that he was making the right choice, and doing what was best.

"Logically, it might have the greatest chance of success," said Reginald. "But intuitively, you're wrong. You can't determine the angels' true intentions with logic. I can't prove it, but I don't think that this is what they'd want."

"How can it not be? They say that we've lost. That the descendants of Cain have been beaten by the descendants of Abel. They say that as long as their chessmen cannot win, they're willing to tip their king and concede. How can we change their minds other than to start *winning the game?*"

"I don't know."

Timken shook his head in disgust, then stood. "You're not using logic. Just like every other stupid person in history, you're using emotion. And just like every other stupid person, you'd lead everyone to their deaths. This is why I had to do what I did. Because people like you won't make the decision that needs to be made."

Reginald stood inside of his cell. He felt strangely powerful, but not physically powerful. He wouldn't be able to overpower Timken or escape, but somehow he was certain that he had the upper hand.

"There's more at play here than logic." And he thought of angels and visits to the minds of others, and he saw the sparks flying from Claire's fingertips.

"You're supposed to be the best mind among us," said Timken, shaking his head.

"I am," said Reginald. "And I'm telling you that you're wrong."

All at once, Timken's conservative, composed exterior shattered. An ugly look crawled across his face. The was a blur as he ran to the corner, skipped up the wall, and ripped the television from its mount. It came out in a shower of plaster and dust. With an inarticulate scream, Timken threw the monitor to the floor hard enough to send metal bits skittering to the four walls. The noise, which was the only one in the soundproofed room, was very loud. Then he stood over the destroyed appliance, his hair a mess, his eyes wild, his suit coat unbuttoned and his shoulders rising and falling with his heavy breaths.

"Is that what logic looks like?" said Reginald, who'd watched the tantrum with a neutral expression, totally nonplussed.

Timken ran a hand over his frazzled hair, smoothing it. Then he buttoned his suit coat, carefully tucking his tie into it.

"I'm not wrong. Our species is facing a crisis, and I'm the only chance to save it."

Reginald shook his head. "They won't let you."

Timken gave a small chuckle. "They won't be able to stop us. We're too strong, too fast, and too intelligent."

"Not the humans. I meant the rest of the Vampire Nation."

This time, Timken actually laughed, then gave Reginald a pitying look. The look said that Reginald was unthinkably naive, and that Timken regretted having to break an unpleasant truth to him.

"I think you're underestimating the power of fear and of denial," he said.

"We'll see," said Reginald, thinking of Maurice, of Nikki, of Karl, and of all of the vampires of the world who would, if push came to shove, learn exactly what Timken was up to. They'd kept their mouths shut to avoid war, but once war became inevitable and the humans began to fight back, all bets would be off. Reginald didn't believe that most vampires would stand back and let it happen. He couldn't. The thought was too terrible... but still, that logical core within him that Timken so wanted the approval of seemed to think that it might be true.

"Yes," said Timken. "We will."

He pulled a pair of gloves from a shelf and put them on. Then he fished a keychain out of his pocket, found a long-barreled key, and walked forward to slide it into the lock on Reginald's cell.

"What are you doing?" said Reginald.

"I'm letting you go."

"Why?"

Timken looked up at him, one gloved hand grasping a smooth silver bar. "It's like I said: it's not a fair fight if my opponent is behind bars."

"We'll tell people what you're doing," said Reginald. And as soon as he'd said it, he could almost feel Maurice's fist punching him in the back of the head. *Get away first. Pontificate, ponder, and gloat second.*

"You'll try. But you're the criminal who just tried to rig an election, and I'm the man who believed so much in the future of the Vampire Nation that he saw your value, recognized that everyone makes mistakes, and had the compassion to give you a second chance."

The door opened. Timken stepped aside, waiting. But at first, Reginald couldn't leave the cell. It was a strange, strange reversal of roles, and one that his mind was actually having trouble processing. Releasing Reginald really would make Timken look better, and keeping him in a cell wouldn't silence his message. The vampire media, which had newly expanded freedoms that matched those of America's press, would want to talk to him if Timken kept him, and when they did, Reginald would give them his crazy, conspiracy theorist's rant.

Maybe he should stay. He'd win a moral victory, and he'd at least have value as a martyr.

But that was stupid. So he stepped into the main room and looked back at the cell, wondering what had just happened.

"You'll see that I'm right," said Timken.

"You're not right."

"Yes," said Timken. "I am. I don't want us to be adversaries, Reginald. I want you on my side. The right side. The *logical* side. The side that is the only chance our species has of surviving. After you have time to think about this, you'll see. And when you do, I will be here ready to welcome you aboard. I will be waiting."

"What you're doing isn't helping us," said Reginald. "It's dooming us."

Timken shrugged. "Are you sure about that? The way I see it, we have two options. We can fight and maybe survive, or we can do nothing and definitely not survive. You saw the Ring of Fire. You heard the angel. You know that apathy will kill us all. I don't want to do what needs doing either, Reginald, but I'll tell you this: I'd take a vampire earth over our extinction."

Reginald didn't respond for a long time. Finally, meeting Timken's eyes, he said, "Yes. I'm sure."

Timken nodded and extended a hand. Reginald had a moment of unreality when he realized that Timken wanted him to shake it. Reginald didn't, and eventually the hand lowered. Timken gave a cordial nod.

"I'll see you on the battlefield," he said.

Then, with no response to give, Reginald walked through the door of the holding area, down a long corridor past at least a dozen checkpoints staffed by red-helmeted soldiers, climbed the steps into the Asbury lobby, and walked out into the cool dark night.

NEXT

There was no further point in hiding. Timken had more or less given Reginald full permission to exist, and tacit approval seemed to have been given to Maurice and Nikki as well. So after Reginald found a cyber cafe and Skyped the others to tell them what had happened and what he'd learned, the remaining two American vampires bid Karl and the others goodbye. Karl promised whatever support he could give and said he'd begin seeding word through whatever friendly channels he still had. These were few and far between. The entire vampire world had seen the video and reports on the rigged American election, and the story needed little embellishment or bias to be damning. The truth was damning enough.

What was worse was that the more he thought about it, Reginald couldn't convince himself that Timken was entirely wrong. Yes, what he had in mind was genocide. Yes, he'd done mass murder. Yes, it was reprehensible and no, no matter what logic there was, Reginald could not agree with his choice or support it. Reginald vowed to fight Timken and his army with every breath remaining in his undead body. But privately, within his own mind, Reginald replayed their encounter and couldn't shake a simple truth: It was possible that Timken was right. Perhaps extermination of the human race was what the angels wanted. Perhaps anything less would result in the extermination of the vampire race. Perhaps, in the end, it really was one or the other. Maybe the time for cohabitation of both halves of the whole that used to be humankind had ended. Maybe there really could no longer be creatures who ruled the day and creatures who, quite separately, ruled the night. If Cain and Abel were real, maybe there'd really been a biblical flood. Maybe there really were powers that none of them understood. Maybe from time to time, the game playing itself out on Earth needed a hard reset, like shaking an Etch-a-Sketch or burning a forest to cinders. Maybe from time to time, nature wanted to clear the slate entirely and start over.

But regardless, the one thing that Reginald was sure of was that if it was "right" to wage the war that was at its tipping point, he wasn't able to be "right." If it meant saving lives, he was quite willing to be wrong.

Despite the fact that they seemed to be safe from Timken and his troops, Nikki and Reginald didn't feel comfortable returning to their old homes. They didn't trust Timken enough to lay their throats right out on the chopping block, and there were also the masses to contend with. Nikki and Maurice could blend in reasonably well, but Reginald stuck out like a sore thumb. As Timken had predicted, popular opinion applauded Timken's compassion in releasing Reginald, but as Reginald had predicted, the masses weren't as compassionate or forgiving. He'd never been liked amongst vampires, but that dislike had reached violent new levels. His house had been vandalized while he'd been gone. He was nearly attacked everywhere they went in public, and when Maurice was recognized, he was attacked as well. So they split the difference. They didn't go home and they didn't continue to hide. Instead, both Reginald and Nikki moved in with Maurice, and so did Reginald's mother and Nikki's sister.

And finally, so did Claire and her mother, Victoria. Claire

suddenly seemed not only precious in and of herself, but also more important than ever. Everyone could feel it.

There was more than enough room for all of them in Maurice's sprawling estate, and a few quick modifications of the grounds turned the entire complex into a well-defended fortress. Maurice hired Brian Nickerson, who was too proud to move in for his own protection, as head of security. Brian moved in with his entire family: his human wife Talia (who had decided to turn imminently instead of waiting as she'd planned, now that vampire bootcamp was out of the question) and his three human children. Brian prowled the grounds, supervising the house's contingent of loyal guards. He brought with him his trademark good humor. In order to appear equally comic and intimidating, he even began wearing sunglasses and an incredibly tight black shirt that read, FUCK WIT ME AND GET YOSEF KILLT.

With so many of them under the same gigantic roof, the house took on the feel of a commune. In a way, it was nice. They were adequately protected and they seldom left — or, thanks to the sheer size of the place, seldom wanted or *needed* to leave. It was easy to forget that there was a hostile world just beyond the gates, and that a war was brewing. They had meals of blood and human food together, as a group. They gathered around fires in Maurice's massive central fireplace, and Claire roasted marshmallows with Brian's still-human children.

When they were alone, Reginald and Nikki let down the guards and happy faces that they held so carefully around the others. Reginald acted happy-go-lucky and uncaring, but behind closed doors he was studying the outside world as he'd never studied it before. He watched every news report he could and devoured all the information out there. He was in constant contact with Karl and struggled to build inroads with other leaders. The going was tough; nobody wanted to associate with a treasonous conspiracy theorist or believe his message: that the now-duly-elected president of the Vampire Nation (the title of "Deacon" had been retired, along with the formality of capitalizing it in print) had masterminded the biggest terrorist event since 9/11 and had genocide in mind. And if they were unreceptive to that message, they were flat-out allergic to Reginald's other message: that the right course of action was to rebel against their beloved leader in order to protect and save humans.

Things between Reginald and Nikki took on an ominous quiet — in their relationship, but also in their moods. Both carried the burden of the world on their shoulders, and it was very heavy.

"How will it begin?" Nikki asked one night. They were sitting in their room in the east wing of Maurice's mansion. It was very different from their room in the catacombs under the Chateau. This one looked like it belonged in Versailles.

Reginald pinched the bridge of his nose and repeated a sentence he was used to and loathed saying: "I don't know."

"Will they try to kill them all?"

"Not all," said Reginald. "Vampires will still need blood. My guess is they'll want to farm them. Like cows for milk."

Nikki flopped back onto the bed.

"We should turn Claire," she said. "To protect her. As a vampire, she'd be safe."

"No," said Reginald.

Nikki looked up, ready to protest, but they'd discussed it over and over and over. Reginald wanted Claire to have a chance to grow up and grow strong, rather than being frozen as a child forever. He knew all too well how it felt to have his growth arrested at an inopportune time.

"Better to be small and alive than dead," she said.

"It's more than that. She's somehow *important*. I can feel it in my blood. She has a role to play, and she needs to be free to become whatever it is that she's supposed to be."

"According to her, you have a role to play too," said Nikki, referring back to Claire's prediction to Balestro back on that German hilltop. "You're supposed to lead."

Reginald laughed. He thought of the few vampires who didn't want him dead. The list was very short.

"She's growing into something," said Reginald. "It's amazing, watching her abilities develop. She's opening somehow... like a flower."

"Mmm," said Nikki. "Poetic."

Reginald closed his eyes. He thought of the signs of war he'd already seen, both at the top of the news in new animosities and below the surface, where only a mind like his could see it. It was coming. It was very, very close. And soon there would be massive bloodshed on both sides, and there was nothing he could do about it.

"I'm scared, Nikki," he said.

She leaned over and put a hand on his knee. "We're safe in here. We'll be fine."

"I'm scared for the world."

Nikki kept her hand where it was for a moment, then removed it.

After a quiet minute, she said to Reginald, "So riddle me this, Batman. You believe that Claire is important. That she's somehow... I don't know... destined for something?"

"Mmm."

"And this *important* person, she believes that you are somehow also destined for something. She told Balestro. 'He will show them the way.' About you."

"She also said 'booga-booga' to him and made jazz hands."

Nikki laughed, remembering how Claire had bullshitted her way through her encounter with the angel. She'd been making it up, but Reginald had predicted that some of what she said held nuggets of truth, and over the past months, he'd come to believe it more and more.

"A lot of it was crap, yes," said Nikki. "But you believe some of it."

"Yes."

"You believe the big stuff. The war. The change. The purge. And you showing them the way."

Reginald thought for a moment before responding. His natural reticence to see himself as important, superior, or relevant wanted to suppress that last part, but the deeper, more intelligent part of himself felt sure that it was true.

"I guess."

"So how can all of that be true without there being a way, somehow, to win in the end?"

Reginald inhaled, exhaled. Then he blinked and looked over at Nikki.

"You're absolutely right."

Nikki smiled. "Of course I am."

"But that doesn't mean that we — and the world — don't have to go through Hell first."

Nikki had stopped listening. She'd won her point and was now content to gloat. "Whateva," she said. "Above my pay grade."

"I'm still scared," he said.

"Of course you are."

"But I guess I just need to trust. Have some faith."

"Sounds like a plan."

"And wait for things to unfold."

"Sure."

Reginald stood up. "Suddenly, for the first time ever, I actually want blood."

Nikki sat up, her face brightening. It was like a sick kid with nausea saying he felt well enough for a cheeseburger. She said, "I'll get you a pouch!" And she started to stand, prepared to make for the kitchen. But Reginald grabbed her by the wrist.

"Vampire blood," he said. And his fangs came out.

"It won't nourish you," said Nikki.

"But it's so arousing," said Reginald, walking into Nikki so that the backs of her calves bumped the bed.

"What kind of a girl do you think I am?"

Reginald answered by using what scant vampire strength he had to grab Nikki and leap with her clasped against him, into the air, and onto the mattress. The support broke away from the bed frame and crashed to the floor. Nikki, crushed beneath him, laughed. And then she showed him what kind of a girl she was.

Outside, beyond the gates, the vampire world bared its fangs.

And seven billion humans — many of them highly armed and ready — lived while they still could, filled with their precious, dangerous blood.

ALSO BY JOHNNY B. TRUANT

Winter Break

Pattern Black

Pretty Killer

Cursed

The Bialy Pimps

Namaste

The Target

La Fleur de Blanc

Axis of Aaron

Devil May Care

Screenplay

The Island

Burnout

Sick and Wired

———

UNICORN WESTERN:

Unicorn Western

The Wanderers

A Fistful of Magic

Shimmer to Yuma

The Man Who Shot Alan Whitney

The Spectacular Seven

Open Meadows

The Unforgotten

The Magic Bunch

Unicorn Genesis

———

FAT VAMPIRE:

Fat Vampire

Fat Vampire 2: Tastes Like Chicken

Fat Vampire 3: All You Can Eat

Fat Vampire 4: Harder Better Fatter Stronger

Fat Vampire 5: Fatpocalypse

Fat Vampire 6: Survival of the Fattest

The Vampire Maurice

Anarchy and Blood

Vampires in the White City

Fangs and Fame

Game of Fangs

———

INVASION:

Invasion

Contact

Colonization

Annihilation

Judgment

Extinction

Resurrection

Save the City

Save the Girl

Save the World

Longshot

———

THE INEVITABLE:

Robot Proletariat

The Infinite Loop

The Hard Reset

Cascade Failure

Reboot

En3my

———

DEAD CITY:

Dead City

Dead Nation

Dead Planet

Dead Zero

Empty Nest

———

THE DREAM ENGINE:

The Dream Engine

The Nightmare Factory

The Ruby Room

The Pandora Core

The Engine Convergence

The Tinkerer's Mainspring

———

GORE POINT:

Gore Point 1

Gore Point 2

Gore Point 3

———

THE BEAM:

The Beam: Season One

The Beam: Season Two

The Beam: Season Three

The Beam Season Four

The Beam Season Five

Future Proof

Plugged

The Future of Sex

———

THE TOMORROW GENE:

The Tomorrow Gene

The Eden Experiment

The Tomorrow Clone

Null Identity

———

COMEDIES:

Everyone Gets Divorced

Greens

Fiends

Decoy Wallet

———

NONFICTION:

The Fiction Formula

Fiction Unboxed

Iterate & Optimize

The Story Solution

Write. Publish. Repeat.

The One With All the Writing Advice